EDITED BY
RUTH ANNA EVANS

Edited by Ruth Anna Evans
Formatted by Hungry Shadow Press
Proofread by Tasha Reynolds and Candace Nola
Art by Ruth Anna Evans
Art edited by Hazel Mayse

www.ruthannaevans.com

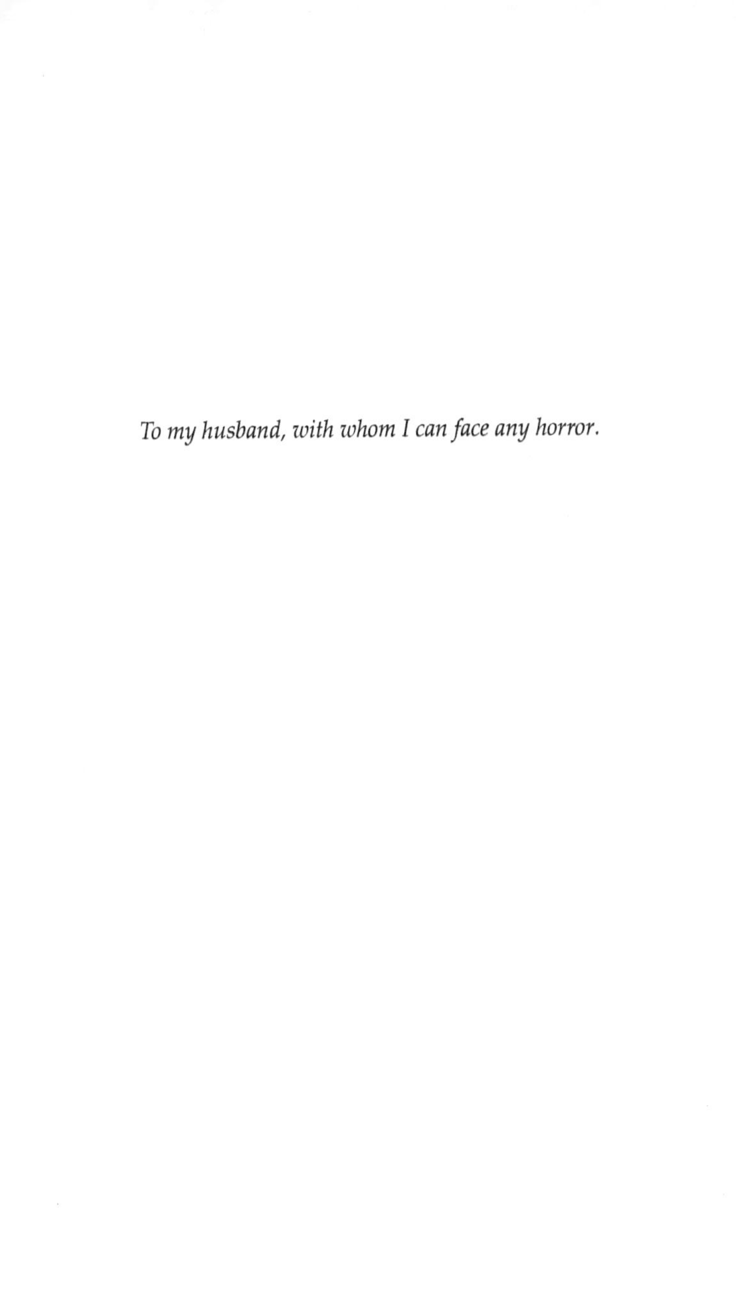

To my husband, with whom I can face any horror.

CONTENTS

CONTENT WARNINGS

Teething: Child loss

The Last Hamburger Restaurant in the World: Just totally disgusting and obscene

Every Part of You: Partner death

If I Carry You: Child suffering

Dr. Parasite: Feces

Family Dinner: Fatphobia

Bitch Witch: Sexuality with uncomfortable elements

FOREWORD

Bridgett Nelson

FOREWORD

BRIDGETT NELSON

I was downright giddy when asked to write the foreword to *OOZE: Little Bursts of Body Horror*, edited by Ruth Anna Evans. As both an avid reader and horror writer, nothing is scarier to me than well-done body horror. Creating this foreword feels like a little gift, and as soon as I was asked, I knew exactly the direction I wanted to take. So, what do you say? Let's do this!

Chickenpox.

I realize many of you have probably never had to deal with the dreaded 'pox, but growing up in the eighties, a week filled with extreme itching and abject misery was a childhood rite of passage. I'm going to share with you a little story, one that highlights the events that triggered my eventual love of body horror.

The year was 1983. I was in second grade. It was a beautiful spring day. My elementary school was having its annual Field Day festivities. For those of you who are unfamiliar, Field Day is an end-of-the-school year affair during which the entire student body participates in various sporting events. Things like relay races, the three-legged race, the water balloon throw, bean bag toss, tug of war, hula-hooping, and various other fun games.

My friend Minda and I decided we'd be partners in the three-legged race, which was one of the first events. We stood side by side and tied our inner ankles together, creating the 'third' leg. We carefully made our way to the starting line, joking and laughing with many of our classmates. The physical education teacher blew the whistle and we were off! Minda and I, who had done this many times before, were in the lead, our three legs working in perfect harmony. We ran across the dew-covered grass and then headed down a gently sloping hill. My sneakers, the soles worn down after the daily wear of an entire school year, slid on the wet grass. Down on my ass I went. Hard. When I fell, I instinctively put my arms down to catch myself, and the right one took the brunt of my weight. I heard it crack.

Minda helped me up, and the physical education teacher checked my arm. There was no bruising, no bones protruding from my skin. Hell, it wasn't even crooked! My parents weren't notified. I wasn't rushed to the ER for x-rays. I stayed and participated in Field Day. When my mom picked me up after school, she immediately noticed how weirdly protective I was of my arm. I explained what happened, and she drove me to the emergency room forty-five minutes northwest of our home.

My arm *was* broken…a type of body horror all its own!

I had a hairline fracture in my radius—a big one. Thankfully, hairline fractures don't require the bone to be set and, even better news, the physician said I could use a leather Velcro cast instead of the plaster version, if I promised to leave it on. I made the promise, but as you will soon find out…I lied.

Frickin' cast.

After my mother gave the school officials a stern

talking to, normal life resumed. That is, until I woke up one week later with red, itchy spots covering virtually every inch of my body. They were *everywhere:* legs, arms, back, chest, neck, toes, eyelids…they were even inside my mouth and nose. I'm not sure I even looked human. Mom herded me into our baby-blue Jeep Renegade and straight to the pediatrician's office. He took one look at my repugnant body and said, "That's the worst case of chickenpox I've ever seen!" Damn right. Even my chickenpox were winners!

Summer was coming to West Virginia, and it was HOT. Back in those days, my dad hadn't yet installed central air/heating in our home. And remember, I had a leather cast covering my arm. Mom, worried the chickenpox needed to 'breathe,' called the doctor. He said if I rested my arm on a pillow and kept it very still, I could take the cast off twice a day and let the rash air out. I felt myself getting nauseous the first time the cast came off. All those itchy pox marks under my sweaty cast had turned into a veritable nightmare. My arm looked like fucking cauliflower. Chickenpox blisters—and make no mistake about it—they *were* blisters, and they *did* leak, had swollen to abnormally large sizes from the heat and moisture beneath my cast. They seemed to be growing one on top of another. I remember thinking, "How is a virus doing this to my skin? I'm a monster! I'm a *monster!*"

Those flesh-colored, fluid-filled sacs triggered my lifelong trypophobia—a repulsion and aversion to irregular patterns or clusters of small holes or bumps. I had no idea what trypophobia was back then…but I totally had it. My arm was vile.

I became obsessed with the blisters. They were so itchy, but I knew I couldn't use my fingers to scratch them…they would have exploded into an unholy mess of clear goop. So, I used my lips. Yeah, yeah. I know. It's gross. But until you've dealt with oozy Gigantor chickenpox, I suggest you withhold judgment. And I have big lips, so they offered the perfect, "Oh my God, that feels so good," gentle scratches.

I'm never going to get another kiss in this lifetime, am I?

Eventually, the chickenpox scabbed over and faded, and my arm looked less like a cruciform vegetable and more like a human appendage. Yet, to this day, especially if I'm cold, you can see the faint purple scars that those hideous chickenpox left on my skin, especially on my inner wrist. They forever marred me.

For those of you who have read my story "Spores," do you get it now?

Years later, I was scrolling through Facebook and came upon a ridiculous article revealing a supposed new form of breast cancer in women. The photo accompanying the article was of a woman's breast, with a lotus pod photoshopped to look like it was growing out of her skin. Can you imagine seeing something like that on your skin? Oh my God. Ack! Despite knowing it was fake, the image was so disturbing to me, I ran to the bathroom and puked. And *that* is when I did a Google search and realized I suffered from trypophobia.

Yep, friends, a lotus pod made me puke. Or maybe it was more the 'lotus pod growing out of a boob' thing. I dunno. But it rattled me.

I'm giving you a lot of 'make fun of Bridgett' material, aren't I?

But here is my truth: I can't think of anything worse than living day to day as my body morphs and turns on me—having no control over the one thing that should offer me complete autonomy. To me, that is genuinely scary shit and why books like *OOZE: Little Bursts of Body Horror* are so integral to the horror culture. Body horror is set apart from so many of the other sub-genres of horror because, on many levels, it is plausible. Not only plausible, but happening every single day to people we know.

While body horror often overlaps other sub-genres of horror, there is a psychological aspect—a vulnerability, perhaps—that defines this category. And horror writers, we love to play on people's vulnerabilities. Muahaha!

Ahem. Moving on…

OOZE: Little Bursts of Body Horror touches on transformation, mutilation, contagion, disease and many other of the body horror tropes we've come to love. The stories are fun, disgusting, and impeccably written. As I was reading this nasty little book, there were times I cringed in revulsion. That, my friends, is the sign of kickass writing.

Cat Voleur's "Proper Contact Maintenance" had me squirming in my seat. Eyeballs, contacts, pain…holy shit, it's intense! "The Last Hamburger Restaurant in the World," written by the incredibly talented Judith Sonnet, is one of the most creative body horror stories I've read… and with a twist! Speaking of Judith, she took home first-place at the KillerCon Gross-Out contest, and I came in second. We'll forever be "the two grossest gals in town." By sharing that anecdote, I'm pointing out that Judith knows gross. And she does it very, *very* well. Another story I found disturbing as hell was "Teething" by Cassandra Daucus. So dark. So vivid. So sad.

If you like body horror, this is the book for you.

So, get a shower, check your skin to verify nothing is growing anywhere it shouldn't be, grab a nice snack (actually, maybe not), and enjoy the Bursts!

I offer just one disclaimer: If, while you're reading this, you get an itch and feel compelled to scratch it with your lips…sorry. My bad.

-Bridgett Nelson
December 30, 2022

INTRODUCTION

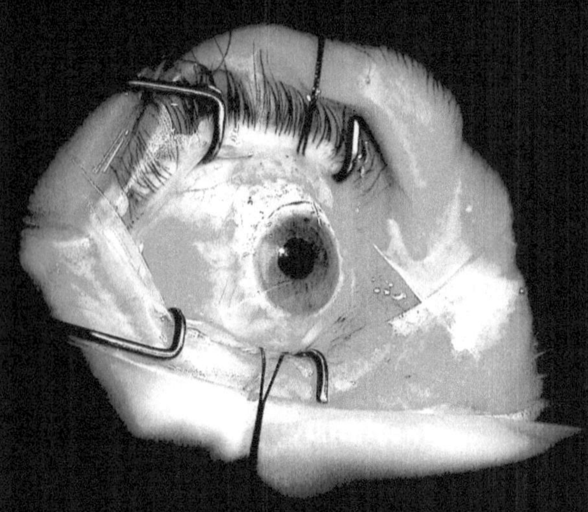

RUTH ANNA EVANS

INTRODUCTION

RUTH ANNA EVANS

I knew I liked writing body horror: how the icky sticky oozy twisty eruptions of nastiness held something special. I would cackle to myself when I made a breast explode or when someone's treatment for her hair loss resulted in boiling blisters all over her scalp and face. It was just fun.

But I didn't know how much I like to read body horror until I spent my entire Christmas break of 2022 reading almost two hundred short short stories filled with utterly delightful takes on "Little Bursts of Body Horror." The best stories were those that I never expected, never would have written myself. And that's the other thing I realized with this little project—making an anthology is a project full of joy, because you get to craft a piece that is full of surprises, even to yourself.

The idea for Ooze was born from an explosion of art that I made as a way of coping with a sudden bipolar episode. All day, every free moment, I was making covers for books no one had yet written. It was how I survived an exceedingly grim and frightening couple of weeks until a medication change rescued me. When it was over, I looked back at a cover I had made, with an eyeball pried open by needles, and thought—there is something here. Something real. Something horrible. I wanted to tap into that, beyond what I was capable of on my own. And so the concept for Ooze was born.

I wanted the stories in Ooze to be short—really short. The kind that when you start reading, you know an ending is smashing its way full speed in your direction, the kind that in just moments lets you know something is terribly, horribly wrong. Short horror is my favorite kind of horror because it makes me more uncomfortable than any other kind. It ricochets around my brain like a bullet, doing untold and permanent damage.

As soon as I had the idea, I knew I wanted Judith Sonnet and Rowland Bercy Jr. to feature. These folks write the nastiest shit I've ever read, but they also have a way with a story, a way of taking you on a short, terrifying roller coaster ride full of plot and pacing and emotion. That's what I wanted. Stories, not sketches. Not just a burst, but a burst of horror. And to me, horror means story. I was so grateful when they both said "Yes".

Lor Gislason's prose made them another obvious invite. *Inside Out* grabs you and holds you and makes you want to read more and more. In *Ooze*, you get a tiny little picture of what they can do, but take this as my overwhelming recommendation to read more.

And Cat Voleur's stories are just so perfect. I haven't read one thing she's written that didn't ring absolutely true. That's what I wanted in this collection—stories that cut through the noise of the media we all consume and hit you where it hurts, make you cringe, shout "NO!", and leave you feeling just that little bit changed.

Then I opened for submissions. I was utterly and completely unprepared for the flow of fantastic stories I was privileged to read. I could have done three anthologies (alas, I am too poor), but let it be known that some of the stories rejected for this project still live in my brain. The ones that were accepted, you will find, are simply stunning. Infestations. Dissolutions. Transformations. Soft horror, gross-out horror. Body horror.

Some of these authors should be household names. Lena Ng's story, *Beauty is in the Eye of the Other,* is so expertly crafted and well-told, you will have to read it more than once just for the pure joy of it.

The first story in this collection, *Teething,* is from Cassandra Daucus, who is a fresh voice in horror publishing. She absolutely knows what she's doing, and I'm proud to publish her at this point in her career. Watch for big things.

I could rave about any and all of the stories in this collection, but the book is supposed to be about little bursts, so I'd better wrap up. You just have to read it. Read to the end; every story is a banger.

Oh, and if you've gotten this far, you have been as delighted as I was to read Bridgett Nelson's foreword, which pulls together the thought of how personal body horror is to each of us. We all have our experiences with our bodies doing things they shouldn't—although we haven't all kissed our own blisters. Gross, Bridgett.

That's what this anthology is. Gross. Fun. Heartfelt. Short. I hope you enjoy it as much as I do, and I hope you support the authors contained herein. And as my mom always used to say when I was puking: "Try not to get any on ya'."

Cassandra Daucus

TEETHING

TEETHING

CASSANDRA DAUCUS

THE BABY IS TEETHING. I cradle it in the crook of my arm, rub my finger across its gum, and will it to give up and sleep. But it won't be soothed. It champs fruitlessly, pushes its pink gums against my fingertip while it squirms and mewls. I stare straight ahead as it bites and sucks, and keep my eyes on the blank square of green-stained drywall so I don't have to look at the baby.

Its face is a little potato, off-colored and misshapen. It smells rotten, like old cheese left in the sun, and its cries are wet gurgles, never loud but always repulsive. The baby disgusts me, even thinking about it makes my gorge rise. And yet I hold it through the night, rubbing its gums and humming lullabies.

I remember being excited at first. The two lines on the stick brought me hope, and the two heartbeats brought me joy. My husband, a twin himself, was thrilled at the prospect of two of his own. But at the next appointment there was only one heartbeat, only one fetus. Only one baby. The doctor said a vanishing twin was common enough, that she would keep her eye on the remaining baby's development, but she didn't expect any issues. My husband insisted it was fine, but I could tell he was lying.

When he left with three months still to go I wasn't surprised.

I continued preparing for the birth. What choice did I have? But every day that passed, every doctor's appointment when I was told the pregnancy was progressing as expected, every blanket and stuffed animal pressed into my hands with a well-meaning smile, I could feel that something was wrong with the baby. And when that baby came out, I knew. I *knew*.

The baby cries louder, its wiggling turning into a thrash. I tighten my hold, rubbing harder against the gum, the hard bone beneath a contrast with the soft pink that covers it. The stench builds with the movement, grows sharper and more intense. The baby stiffens and squeals, a loud, long sound that reminds me of a train braking. The noise is cut short by a squelching pop, and the baby goes limp, my fingers still held loosely in the wet warmth of its revolting little mouth.

Although the body is still, something moves inside it, wriggling under the surface of its belly, its neck, the soft spot at the crown of its head. I hold my breath and wait to see what will happen next. Only a moment later, the silence is broken by a wet crunch.

In the bloody ruins of the baby's jaw my finger meets a new obstacle. Not a tooth, hard and sharp, but something warm and soft. I stroke against it and it moves, pushing further through the hole, reaching for me, a rosebud seeking the sun. Another appears beside it, and another, until eventually there are five of them - five perfect little fingers digging through the gums of her mutilated sibling.

I knew she was in there—the other baby. *My* baby. My baby is ready to be born, and I am honored to be her midwife. The other baby's mouth is small, but so are my hands. I get my second hand in there without too much trouble, say a little prayer, and then I *pull*.

Inspired by H. P. Lovecraft, M. R. James, Shirley Jackson, Robert Aickman, and a ton of fan fiction, Cassandra Daucus (she/her) writes soft horror and dark romance. She is intrigued by how the human mind responds to the unknown, and also enjoys a good gross-out. She is the author of the horror collection, The House on the Beach and The Unicorn, and has published drabbles in Trembling With Fear. Cassandra lives outside of Philadelphia with her family and three cats. She tweets at @residualdreamin and tumbles at https://residualdreams.tumblr.com/.

Five Easy Exercises

You Can Do At Home

TOM COOMBE

FIVE EASY EXERCISES YOU CAN DO AT HOME

TOM COOMBE

GOOD MORNING, Formation Fitness Fam!

If you're reading this, it means you've finished our reFormation program. Please take a moment to pat yourself on your back. As a reFormation graduate, I know how trying these last two months have been. However, this is no time to rest on your laurels. As we always say, there aren't many rest stops on the road to fitness, especially now as we ramp things up towards our Greater Purpose. Besides, with the quarantine period mandated by our medical staff and the latest air quality warning ("Yellow" for much of June and July, if you trust the weather service), you won't be going anywhere for the next few weeks.

While you wait, here are five easy exercises you can do at home to help prepare you for the next stage of your fitness journey.

1. PUSH-UPS

When I finished reFormation, I didn't feel like doing much of anything. Derek was at the office more than usual, the kids weren't much help around the house, and the latest season of *Fixer Upper* seemed a lot more enticing than getting back into my workout routine. I dug myself out of this rut by starting with these simple (but effective) exercises. One set of fifty push-ups will help strengthen your core. Don't cheat yourself by anchoring your legs under a chair.

Remember to hydrate after each workout. Tap water will do in a pinch (although why are you drinking fluoridated government water?) but we recommend our Formation Fitness brand bottled water. We've left a couple of cases in your kitchen. Avoid energy drinks, as you'll find it's now much, much harder for your body to process sugar.

2. RUNNING IN PLACE

You should plan on doing a lot of running when we're in D.C. in November. We know many of you enjoy jogging, and while that's not possible during quarantine, this exercise provides you with many of the same benefits.

To run in place, lift your right arms and left foot at the same time and raise your knee so it's as high as your hips. From there, switch to the opposite foot, bringing your right foot to hip height, while moving your right arms back and your left arms forward and up.

I find that listening to music helps pass the time on these runs. Be sure to consult our list of approved and forbidden songwriters.

3. PLYO PUSH-UPS

Also known as "clap pushups," this exercise is designed to strengthen your chest, abdominals, shoulders, and triceps. Start in the high plank position, with your torso in a straight line, your core tight and your palms right below your shoulder. Lower your body until your chest is almost on the floor. When you push back up, use enough force so that your hands leave the ground. Some people clap as they do this, but don't feel obligated. Plyo push-ups are not a beginner's exercise, but with your experience – and your new arms – it shouldn't be much of a challenge.

I don't know about you all, but I love my new arms. Bryson and Kaylee were scared of them when I came home from the Formation Clinic, and Derek insisted I kept them covered when we ate. I need to remind myself I did this for them, just as you entered the program for your family. Keep that in mind if these six weeks begin to feel like too much, and remember our motto: We must better ourselves for the betterment of our children and of our community.

4. CRAB WALKS

This exercise improves your balance, works your abs, and strengthens your upper body, all of which will be important when we go to D.C. this fall to carry out our Greater Purpose.

Start by sitting on the floor, keeping your feet hip-distance apart. Your arms should be behind your back, fingers aimed forward. Boost yourself off the floor, keeping your abs tight, and begin to "walk": left hands, right foot, right hands, left foot, moving four steps forward and four steps back. This will be a good time to practice your owl neck stretches from last week. These will allow you to look forward during your crab walk, even as the rest of you is moving backward.

5. ELBOW BENDS

Isn't it a blessing to discover the new things your body can do? You'll perform this exercise by holding your arms—your birth arms and your new arms—out in front of you, your hands in a karate chop position. Bend each hand downward at the wrist, putting as much pressure as possible on your forearm muscles until your elbows splinter and pop as your new joints knit themselves into place.

I'll be blunt, Formation Fam: this was the worst pain I've ever experienced. Multiply my eighth-grade appendicitis by the births of both my children and it's still not close. When that first crack came, every nerve above my waist sang like a holy choir. The world turned gray as sweat saturated my workout clothes. The previous night's grilled chicken erupted from my belly onto the floor of our workout room. (Word of advice: if this happens to you, do not look at what is in your vomit.)

My consciousness abandoned me with the second crack, a horrible dry-tree-branch snap. I woke up on my stomach, my arms twisted beneath me at strange angles. The pressure on my elbows was unbearable but the thought of pushing myself up with my broken limbs made me weep. At the moment, my friends, I admit I questioned our Reformation and our Great Purpose. No, that's not true. I denounced them. I would have given everything I worked for to the first person to take away even a little of the pain.

Warm light caressed my face then, far brighter than my workout room's lamp. A still, small voice called my name, so loving and commanding I had to see who it was.

I opened my eyes to find Our Lord stooping to lift me into His arms.

This was not the bony Christ of Catholic churches, but a true carpenter, His hands cracked and leathery with work. His arms were those of a man who had felled trees and hauled stone, and not the arms of a hungry drifter who struggled to carry His cross.

Cradling me like a baby in one arm, He dipped His hand into His wounded side, massaging His blood deep into my screaming joints. His touch cooled my skin like night air.

"Fear not," He whispered as I drifted off. "They will follow you. No matter how many die, they will all follow you."

When I woke, the pain had vanished. I found—as you will—that my elbow joints can swing like saloon doors. I spent the afternoon reveling in the range of motion my new muscles have given me, and not even the sobbing of my children was enough to dampen that blessed feeling.

And this *is* a blessing. It doesn't matter what the woke mob on Facebook says. It doesn't matter what your husband tells his lawyers. It doesn't matter that the inspectors from the health department keep coming around. They'll all see, very soon, once we visit Washington and carry out our Great Purpose. They say the body is a temple, but you've turned yours into a great and holy cathedral. And like any cathedral, it demands worship.

Have a blessed week, Fam. You've got this!

Ainsley Weichrein
Owner/President, Formation Fitness

Tom Coombe is a horror writer whose stories have appeared in Not Deer Magazine, Cemetery Gates Society and a number of recent anthologies. He lives in Pennsylvania's Lehigh Valley with his girlfriend and their demonic cat.

The Last Hamburger Restaurant

Restaurant

In the World

Judith Sonnet

THE LAST HAMBURGER RESTAURANT IN THE WORLD

JUDITH SONNET

"I'M GETTING KIND OF HUNGRY." Chance said.

"There's still trail mix." Martha said.

Chance shuddered. If he ate another shrunken raisin, he was certain he'd throw it back up. Martha always brought too much of that stuff along whenever they went on road trips.

Sherri stuck her head between the front seats and said: "I'm literally starving!"

Chance sighed. It was decided. They needed food and they needed it now. The last thing he wanted to deal with was a hungry teen. Sherri was a good girl, but she could get snippy when her belly was empty. Chance figured he had been the same way when he was sixteen, but that felt like lightyears ago. At fifty, Chance's appetite had dimmed, as had his ability to tolerate petty bullshit. If Sherri was hungry then—by God—he'd feed her.

All Chance wanted for himself was to taste something other than salty M&M's and dried fruit.

Serendipitously, a road sign caught his eye. It was a wooden board with a hamburger painted in its center. The cartoonish meal was dripping with fat bulbs of juice and ketchup. It almost looked like blood, which somehow churned Chance's stomach in a favorable direction. Circling the burger in fancy script was a strange phrase. He read it out loud to his family:

"*The Last Hamburger Restaurant in the World.*" Chance snorted. "Weird name."

"Maybe it's supposed to be ironic. Either way, we should definitely stop there." Sherri said from the back seat. She was leaning back now, putting her knees against Martha's backrest. Martha never complained, even though Chance knew that the teen's knobby knees pressing into her spine through the seat vexed her.

"Put your legs down, hun." Chance said.

Exhaling, Sherri sat up straight.

"Okay. We'll definitely swing by. I could use a burger." Chance said. He scanned the sign as their car whisked by. "It's going to be the next right exit. Keep your eyes peeled, ladies."

They didn't have far to drive. The hamburger joint sat by the side of the road. There was a gravel deposit that served as a parking lot. The eatery's weirdly long name was packed into a too small sign on its front. The building would have looked inconspicuous were it not isolated in the desert. With its beige walls, squat entrance, and lack of flourish, it looked like a cube dropped in a sandbox.

"Huh." Martha said, flummoxed by the appearance of the restaurant. "It's definitely…unique."

Unique in a non-unique way. Chance mulled the contradiction around in his head. He turned the wheel and allowed the car to drift into the surprisingly crowded lot. He caught sight of several confederate flags, a few crass bumper stickers, and a couple shotgun racks on the pickups that filled the lot.

Hopefully no one catches my Bernie sticker. Chase thought. It probably wouldn't happen. The political stamp had been faded by exposure. It was also peeling through the middle.

"Welp. We're here." Chance said.

"This place better not be grungy." Sherri moaned.

"Yeah. I hope their bathrooms are clean." Martha said with a whimper. She had been forced to squat behind a bush a day ago and had made it clear to Chance that she didn't want to repeat the procedure.

Chance decided to hold his tongue. He suspected that both girls would be disappointed by the bathrooms. This was, after all, a redneck burger joint lost in the sands of the desert. He doubted they even had visits from health inspectors.

Chance held the door open and allowed his wife and daughter to enter ahead of him. He took one last glance at the parking lot before following behind them. The cars all looked neglected and dusty. He was shocked to see the nearest pickup didn't have a windshield. *How do you drive in the desert like that?* Chance imagined bits of sand pelting his eyes. It made him shudder.

He walked into the restaurant and let the door clatter closed behind him.

Thankfully, the interior of *The Last Hamburger Restaurant in the World* was more welcoming than the exterior. There were checkered tablecloths, clean floors, and smiling faces. Instead of an angry group of rednecks, the patrons were all blue-collar gentlemen and their families. A few kids screeched and hollered, but their din was acceptable. At least there wasn't a godawful "play place". Chance had always found those tacky.

A waitress with a wide smile and glittery eyes strolled toward Chance and his family.

"Howdy, y'all! Take a seat wherever ya like and I'll be with ya in a jiffy!"

"Thank you." Chance peeked at the nametag on her ample bosom. "Dolly."

Dolly's smile didn't waver as she walked a platter of

steaming burgers toward a table lined with hungry mouths.

"Hey, this place ain't half bad!" Chance said.

"I'm gonna run to the restroom. Order me a Coke, okay?" Martha waddled away.

Sherri and Chance took a table near the far corner of the restaurant. There were menus already laid out, and Chance was happy to note that their surfaces weren't gunky.

"I think we lucked out, Dad." Sherri grinned.

"Yeah. Me too. Now, let's see what we're dealing with here." He scanned the menu.

Dolly approached the table with a lady-bug shaped notepad. "What can I get you folks ta drink?" She asked.

"Coke for the missus." Chance said.

"Root beer for me." Sherri interjected.

"And I'll just do a water. No ice."

Dolly marked her notepad, even though their orders were simple. "Know what y'all wanna eat today or need a moment?"

"Just a second." Chance said.

"All right. Well, I'll be back with yer drinks as soon as possible." Dolly chittered before bounding off. Chance realized he had no clue what age she was. She was locked somewhere between her late twenties and early fifties.

Martha came back and sat at the table. "Sherri, if you need a bathroom… this is probably the best we'll see for hours."

"Really? Huh. This place is a gem!" Chance snickered. "Maybe the foods terrible, who knows?"

"Color me surprised." Martha said with relief. "I expected a greasy spoon."

They examined their menus mutely. When Dolly came back, they were ready.

"I'll take a cheeseburger with mushrooms. Can I get Swiss cheese on it?" Sherri asked.

"Sure, sure." Dolly nodded.

"And cheesy fries."

"Just a side of cheesy fries for me." Martha said. She was stuffed with trail mix, Chance supposed.

"A double cheeseburger with onion rings for me, Thank you." Chance said

"Alrighty, folks! We'll have that out in no time at all!" Dolly smiled. Her teeth were so straight they reminded Chance of a horse's mouth. He curiously wondered what it would be like to be bitten by her. Would her chompers sink in deep or just nick the flesh—

Where had that thought come from? Chance felt somewhat repulsed.

Dolly brought their drinks out shortly thereafter. Sipping his water, Chance tried to focus on anything other than his hungry belly. He watched as happy patrons chowed down on fat burgers. Their clean faces were marred with mustard stains and blobs of gooey ketchup. He watched as Dolly brought a tall milkshake out to a young couple, who shared it with two straws.

"This place is charming as hell." Chance muttered.

Martha whapped his arm. "Don't swear, sweetie."

"I mean it. It feels like what I thought all American diners were like when I was a kid." He smiled. "I've gotta ask her about that name, though."

"It's a weird one, all right." Sherri said.

When Dolly eventually came around with their orders, Chance said: "How'd this place get its name?"

Dolly flashed him a perky smile before saying: "It's a little bit literal."

"Huh?" Chance asked before looking down at his plate. The onion rings were sizzling with grease and the burger looked as if it had been slicked in butter. His heart ached but his belly warbled with excitement. He looked back up, hoping for more of an explanation. Unfortunately, Dolly was already gone.

Chance picked his burger up and took a bite. He expected his taste buds to be soaked with flavor and sauce. Instead, his throat clicked closed and he gave into a retching cough. He spat out a glop of mucoid matter onto his plate. It lay like an exhumed polyp atop his onion rings.

Shocked, mortified, and disturbed, Chance's jaw fell open.

The mass was festering with maggots. They trundled in frilly rows along the spots where his teeth had dug into the meat. It looked as if he had taken a chunk of roadkill and spewed it onto his plate.

"What's the matter? Did you swallow wrong?" Martha asked around a mouthful of cheesy fries.

Coughing, Chance took his glass of water and slurped down a mouthful. It no longer tasted smooth and cool. The water had turned acerbic. He sputtered in revulsion.

"Jesus, Dad. You okay?" Sherri asked, cramming her own burger into her maw.

"That was... that was..." Chance slurred as he looked back at his plate.

A glob of spat-up meat lay on his onion rings. It wasn't covered in mucus and worms. It was just a chunk of mushed burger meat.

Chance picked his burger up and examined it carefully. There was nothing out of the ordinary about it. The burger was, by all intents and purposes, a fine piece of meat.

"Somethin' the matter, hun?" Dolly asked, returning seemingly out of thin air.

"I... yeah." Chance said through clenched teeth. "Something was wrong with my—"

"Nothing wrong with mine." Sherri said before stuffing her face once more.

Chance almost shrieked.

Sherri's burger had changed. It wasn't a piece of meat anymore. It had become a log of wet and clumpy shit.

Wrapped in Swiss cheese, the turd squelched as her teeth clamped over it. He watched as a murky dewdrop of fecal fluid drained down her chin and landed on the checkered tablecloth.

Not only could Chance see that it was feces… he could smell it too. A rank odor fell from his daughter's mouth and stained the air. He gagged at the rancid smell. Turning back toward Dolly, Chance asked:

"What's happening?"

"I don't know how to answer that, sir." Dolly said, her face knitted with concern. 'How about a refill on yer water, though?"

Before Chance could answer, she picked his glass up. Stepping back, Dolly spread her legs. She rucked her skirt up and posed his cup beneath her sex.

If Chance had once thought Dolly beautiful, the sight of her rotten vagina was enough to make him reconsider. Her cunt was gummed with green discharge. Boils grew along the lips of her vagina like bats clinging to the walls of a wet cave. A torrent of diseased urine fell out from her gate and splattered into Chance's cup. He watched as she filled it to the brim with a brackish liquid.

Diligently, Dolly placed the glass back on the table in front of Chance's plate.

"Anything else I can getcha, hun?" Dolly asked with a smile. Her teeth, much like the burgers, had changed. They were now lined with yellow calk, and they ended in sharpened hooks. As if she had taken a nail file to her enamel.

Chance looked away from her. He was too frightened to maintain eye contact.

He caught sight of a man's nose exploding with snot. A spiraling tentacle dangled out from his nostril, pushing a load of green goop out onto his plate. He took a fry, dabbed it in the gunk, then raised it up to his mouth. The tentacle clung to his fingers after he had deposited the snot-wetted fry into his smiling face.

Two kids ran by Chance's table. One's eyes dangled from their sockets, connected only by tenuous optic nerves. The other child's tongue was inflated like a balloon. It broke the child's lower jaw, causing blood to flow down her busted cheeks. She didn't seem to be in any sort of pain, despite the malformation of her mouth.

Blinking rapidly, Chance wondered if he was hallucinating. Maybe, he had fallen asleep at the wheel, and this was some sort of demented dream.

Confused, terrified, and still unable to work past the nasty textures on his taste buds, Chance considered running. One look around the restaurant proved that such efforts would be futile.

The customers were melting together. He watched as the milkshake-sipping couple pressed their heads together. Their heads meshed like wet clay, dripping gobs of rejected flesh into their shake, only to slurp them back up through their straws. Their lips became an entangled vortex, lined with sharpened teeth.

A woman picked her baby up from his stroller and cooed at him, before laying him down on the table and digging her fingers into his stomach. The baby mewled pathetically as her digits broke through his skin and upheaved clumps of internal mush. The baby's arms and legs squirmed against its own mother, but she shoveled a handful of gory matter into her maw. She chewed slowly and laboriously, as if she had never eaten before and would never eat again.

Chance began to scream. He was finally convinced—as the smell of blood wafted over from the dying baby and toward his table—that this was no nightmare.

"Dad, what's the matter?" Sherri's voice sounded distant and muted. It was as if she was speaking underwater.

Chance reached out to take her wrist. He was going to pull her out from this hellish place.

His fingers wrapped around something wet and boneless. Chance's eyes enlarged when he took in what had become of his daughter.

Sherri's skin was sloughing away from her muscles, exposing the red meat beneath her beautiful face and smooth flesh. A row of jutting, yellow teeth cracked out from her jaw. Her real pearly whites fell down in a hailstorm onto her fetid plate of food.

She turned her head toward her father. A vibrating noise gurgled from her collapsing throat, just as the dome of her skull melted like wax.

"I'm… not… hungry… any… *more*…"

All around him, the restaurant fell into chaos.

Fluids exploded from bursting bodies. Gummy strands of mucus dripped from the walls and clung to whatever it touched. Chance wailed in panic and pain as his own seat began to consume him. He felt a leathery substance crawl over his skin, searing it away with invisible teeth.

"I'm… full…" Martha moaned before her own head exploded. The pressurized blow lobbed bits of brain and fragments of skull across the table.

Chance shrieked one last time before a tube snaked around his head and filled his mouth. The tube—which had sprung from the back of Chance's seat—began to pump a viscous fluid into his throat. His eyes rolled into his skull and his esophagus expanded beyond its limits. Chance realized that he was being filled like a condom. Eventually, whatever was filling him would go too far… and he would break apart and join the fluids that carpeted the once spotless floor.

He also realized that the fluid being poured down his gullet was ketchup. Loads and loads… of ketchup.

Once everyone inside the restaurant was digested, the building worked its way up to its feet. Each trunk-like limb was padded with thick fur and lined with curved talons. It made no sound as it moved. Its breathing was so slight, it sounded like a distant gust of wind. It's double-door mandibles leaked blood-laced drool, but it emitted no roars or barks.

Gradually, the restaurant began to walk back into the desert. This meal had been a good one, and its belly was full.

Before long, *The Last Hamburger Restaurant in the World* would be hungry again.

It would come out of hiding, sit down by the road… and it would wait.

†

Judith Sonnet was born in Missouri but now lives in Utah, where she spends her time reading and writing graphic horror stories. The author of No One Rides For Free, Blood Suck, and Torture the Sinners!, she does not hold back on violence or gore! Sonnet is a queer woman, a vegetarian, and a huge fan of 70's cinema.

Every
Part
of You
Lyndsey Croal

EVERY PART OF YOU

LYNDSEY CROAL

FIRST, I remove your eyes, then place the spider eggs in your skull, nestled safely in the empty sockets. Your eyes were so beautiful before, but now they're dark, hollow. It doesn't take long for the spiders to hatch within, then escape and cluster along the edges of your jaw, creating an ever-moving smile. As they grow, they creep across your pale thin face and weave silk across your cheekbones, making them full again. The spiders wait, hungry, as the flies that buzz around your body are caught, their sacs forming dimples under your cheeks. Soon there are many, filling the cavities and spaces between your features. Long, thin legs stretch out from your eyes, winking and blinking in a strange rhythm. I gaze into them for a long time, remembering how yours used to look at me. The way they never faltered when I spoke, or how they narrowed when you knew I was talking nonsense but didn't let on in any other way. The way they didn't shed a tear when we first got the diagnosis, and how they looked to me instead to check if I was okay, even when you were the one who was dying.

As spiders crawl up and down your throat, I think of the way your mouth whispered words so carefully, how almost everything you said was tender, had meaning. Now your voice is a gentle thrum, the scurry of a thousand legs.

⁂

I replace your lungs with caterpillars, resting snug in your broken ribs. They slither between leftover muscle and sinew and feed on the leaves I place in your chest cavity. When they've had their fill, I watch them burrow and begin their metamorphosis, form chrysalises where your lungs once were, dozens of them immobilized. I think of how I waited by your side for so long as you slept, how I couldn't move in case I missed you taking your last breath.

When the moths finally emerge, they flutter between your rib cage, whirring as if you are breathing once more. And I can imagine your breath on my neck, the smell of coffee and honey, the way you inhaled so sharply just after you asked me to marry you and only let it go when I replied. How in that moment of held breath, I could hear your heart beating so fast. And all I wanted to do was to tell you not to worry, that of course, *of course*, the answer was yes. Because I wanted to be with you, always.

Above the moths, I release a swarm of bees and they buzz in your chest, form honey structures around your once-beating heart. Their wings hum in rhythm with my own pulse and I listen to it for a long time, remembering how yours used to race whenever we kissed, danced, lay together, laughed. The way that in your final days I would lie with my head on your chest just to hear it still beating.

⁂

The worms I drop in the soil in your abdomen. They squirm within and I remember how you used to say that the stomach is the way to the heart, and so I take care feeding them. Just like I did for you, carefully, in those last days. Soon, they're fat and wriggling, so alive that I have almost forgotten that there are only bones and rotting flesh beneath. For you are coming together again, my love, dissected and recomposed with the worms, spiders, moths, and bees—more whole every day. More alive every day.

I let loose an army of ants up your arms and legs, and they march from your toes to your femur, fingertips to shoulder blades, forming nests along the crevices of your joints. They are so packed together it looks like your muscles are coming back, and that soon you might stand up strong and take my hand and lift me in your arms once again, and we'd dance and dance like we did on our wedding day, at ceilidhs, or even in our kitchen on quiet evenings when it was just the two of us, until our bodies ached with the thrill of the movement.

There are ladybirds living where your freckles once marked your body, clinging to your carapace, bringing color to your paleness. I used to map your freckles, from top to bottom, and I knew them like they were constellations in the sky—each one unique to you. You were always beautiful, and so you remain, even if you have a new rhythm now, of moving freckles like satellites dancing between stars.

I look now at the wings of the moth, the antennae of the ants, the fangs of the spiders, the spots of the ladybirds, the markings of the bees—all things of perfect symmetry. They are like you and I, you see. Two parts of a whole. Synchronized. Balanced.

You once said you could not live without me. How selfish of you to think I could do the same without you.

When we are done, I lie beside you, take your hand in mine. The insects crawl from you to me—spiders in my hair and ladybirds in my throat. Finally, we are together once more, and I can feel your moth-wing breath, your ant-march touch, the bee-buzz beat of your heart. Oh, how I have missed you, my love, every part.

⌁

Lyndsey Croal (she/her) is an Edinburgh-based author of speculative and strange fiction. She is a Scottish Book Trust New Writers Awardee, British Fantasy Award Finalist, and a LOHF Writers Grant Recipient. Her work has appeared or is forthcoming in over fifty publications, including Mslexia's Best Women's Short Fiction 2021, Dark Matter Magazine, and Orion's Belt. Her debut audio drama "Daughter of Fire and Water" was produced by Alternative Stories & Fake Realities. Her novelette "Have You Decided on Your Question" is published in April 2023 with Shortwave Publishing. Find her on Twitter as @writerlynds or via her website www.lyndseycroal.co.uk.

OSCULUM

D. Matthew Urban

OSCULUM

D. MATTHEW URBAN

SWAYING ON THE DANCE FLOOR, bathed in red light, Julian leans forward, and quick as the thought takes shape in Kathy's mind—*finally, finally*—his lips are on hers, pressing at first very lightly as if against a rotted-out wall ready to crumble at the slightest touch, then more firmly, gradually more firmly as his face moves closer, his lips' aperture opening, and she returns the pressure, answers the increase, so that his lips deform under the impulse of hers and hers under his, closeness pushing their mouths open, *finally, finally*, her tongue moving across his lips, his teeth, his tongue pushing against hers, his teeth hard against her lips, bony, unsheathed, harder and harder, she grips the back of his head, his hair curling between her fingers, she pulls him forward, his hands on her face, palms riding a thin tide of sweat across her cheeks to the sides of her head, each bringing the other closer, pulling the other in, teeth hard against teeth as if no lips interposed, and now is when she first tastes blood, the dark tang of it sliding between their tongues so that she doesn't know if it's her blood or his, now he first starts to make a sound, a whining sound like a dog smelling a stranger, now she feels new wetness and a sting in her lips as the teeth begin to press through, hard edges into red flesh, her own teeth entering her lips from behind as a cloud of red liquid light fills her mouth and she pulls him closer and he pulls her closer, pain rushing and roaring in her mouth, teeth pressing directly on teeth as her fingers clutch his head so tight her nails dig into his scalp, his hands squeezing her head as if seeking to meet in the middle of her brain, hands pulling heads ever closer, further, and her eyes that have been squeezed shut now open and flow, two hot cataracts gushing down her cheeks as her eyes roll in ecstatic terror, *what's happening, why are we doing this*, she sees his open eyes flashing, reflecting red light, more radiant with fear than with light, she hears herself making noises, sounding like a crushed animal, panic explodes from his weeping, bloodshot eyes, panic piercing her own eyes to thunder and echo in her brain, *please, please, please, please*, her eyes rolling, frantic, the room flashing red around her, the dance floor crammed with bodies pressed together, red-lit fountains pouring from heads mashed against heads, hands tangled around hands like lumps of crumpled wire as her hands now crumple, her fingers snap and fold, not feeling like fingers anymore, drooping and twisting, his fingers popping like firecrackers behind her ears, what were hands now jagged shards wrapped in meat, the meat always there, hidden, now exposed, inescapable, horror and pain and wild delight swirling in her brain like the hot blood and meat that swirl in her mouth as her teeth shatter and his mouth enters hers, the stumps and spears of his wrecked teeth raking her gums, her burst, streaming tongue flapping against the crushed pulp that was his lips, flapping like a burning flag as their faces begin to collapse, noses and chins buckling under the unbearable, ever more unbearable, pressure, blood pouring from all over, their faces two torn, flowing masses, one mass, one flesh, and the thought howls in her mind as their voices are howling, gurgling howls through gags of meat and blood, bubbling in springs of blood, *love is union, love is union*, red light falling on red blood falling on red flesh falling into itself, falling into absolute union, selfsame, red and red and red and red and red.

D. Matthew Urban hails from Texas and now lives in Queens, New York, where he reads weird books, watches weird movies, and writes weird fiction. His stories have appeared in Dose of Dread (Dread Stone Press), Shredded (Cursed Morsels Press), and The Theatre Phantasmagoria (Night Terror Novels), among other venues. He can be found on Twitter @breathinghead.

A New Kind
of Meat
BRANDON APPLEGATE

A NEW KIND OF MEAT

BRANDON APPLEGATE

"DELICIOUS," David says through his mouthful of boiled flesh. He brings a napkin to his lips and stains it with crimson broth.

"Oh, good!" Miranda smiles and takes another bite of toast.

"No stew?" he asks.

"I'm not that hungry, and besides, you know I want to keep my figure for you, dear. But you need your strength," she chides.

David allows himself a small, private smile. Miranda has been sullen of late. It's pleasant to see her in good spirits. She's perfect when she's happy. She'd had no choice in the beginning—he'd showered her with praise and gifts, and she'd responded like they always do. It was effort, but she'd been worth it. A wizard in the kitchen and a tigress in the sack. Not an inch of sag or cellulite, a spotless house, and miraculous food.

"Your loss," he says. "Peter's, too—where is the boy, anyway?"

"Oh—he said something about working on a project with a friend. Won't be back until late."

"I've never known the little layabout to *work* on anything." David snorts. Either Miranda is full of shit, or Peter is; he's not sure which. He'd had such high hopes for his son, but all the boy does is play video games, spend money he didn't earn, and order Miranda around like she's hired help. As though he had the right. He's not her husband. But what can be done about it? Raising children is a mother's job, and Peter doesn't have one of those anymore.

It had been unfortunate, but necessary.

Deep water. Ropes. Cinder blocks. Red swirls floating in the black. Decay for her, freedom for him.

Miranda stares at her toast.

"What's wrong, love?" David asks.

She doesn't answer.

"Miranda," he says. Flat, because it's a command, not a question.

She jerks and bumps the table with her knee. Broth sloshes out of his bowl. "Oh! Oh, dear, I'm so sorry. I was just thinking—"

"Well, quit thinking and get a towel!" David roars. "It's all over my shirt!"

Miranda bustles off toward the kitchen.

"Son of a bitch," David barks.

Useless. Everything with tits is useless.

"I'm so sorry, sweetheart." Miranda kneels in front of him with a damp towel and dabs at the blood-red stain.

"Jesus Christ, do you really think you're going to get red broth out of a white shirt with a fucking towel?"

David grabs his shirt plackets and yanks, buttons detaching with firecracker pops, clattering like scattered marbles.

"It's ruined, you stupid bitch!" He wads the shirt and hurls it at her.

Miranda is on her ass, crawling backward, away. Good. Fear is healthy for people like her. They lock eyes, chests heaving. David is the first to turn away. He doesn't have to tell her to leave. She scoops up the ruined shirt and skitters off, a frightened mouse.

With her out of the room, David feels better. His appetite returns.

He scoops the last of the stew into his bowl and sits at the table, shirtless.

"More for me," he grunts, and shovels down more meat.

⊓⌐

David's stomach lurches and leaps, and he grabs it to hold it still. He barely made it to bed, only got to gaze at Miranda's perfect face for a moment, before having to turn around and stagger to the bathroom. Apologies will have to wait.

"Bitch better not—have poisoned—me," he grumbles between acrid, wet burps.

Pain wracks his abdomen, and he falls to his knees. His fingers clutch at his gut. Rancid dinner boils in his throat.

Just have to make it to the toilet.

He crawls. Cold sweat springs to the skin on his arms, forehead, cheeks. Was the meat spoiled? He's abstained from really hitting Miranda so far, only a tap here and there, but when this is over he's going to beat her senseless.

The bathroom's fluorescent glow is blinding. Light rings in his ears. He shuts his eyes. But he's close, and soon his palms slap cold tile.

The stew springs from his bowels into his esophagus. Half-chewed strands of bile-slicked meat jump and lick at the base of his tongue. He gags.

Just a couple of feet from the commode, he heaves. The pain is immense. Red creeps in at the edges of his vision. He's a hose, attached to a terrible hydrant. Red splashes over pristine white tile, splatters up onto the sheetrock in heavy droplets. Chunks of gray, masticated flesh ride the liquid waves and gather at the base of the toilet, against the baseboards.

The pressure eases, and he gasps, on all fours, yellow drool hanging from his trembling lips. Tears sting his eyes. Then it's on again, and he's heaving.

Time ceases. There is only the fire in his gut, the muscular clench as he ejects. Eyes bulge. His ears sing a single high-pitched tone. There is no room for screaming, only for the involuntary and helpless moan that escapes him.

Then it's over again, for at least a moment, and he collapses onto his side. Every muscle aches. Throbbing pain balloons inside his skull.

Miranda stands in the doorway, a crystalline ghost in her white satin nightgown. She is smiling.

David reaches a vomit-soaked hand toward her. *Help me*, he mouths, but his vocal cords lie still.

Miranda laughs.

"Silly boys," she says. "Think they're all big and strong, then they get a little sick, and it's all 'help me' and 'it hurts.'"

She steps into the bathroom and stops before she gets to the puddle David lies in, then squats next to him. David doesn't see the ax until she drops its head onto the floor, her porcelain fingers gripping the end of the handle.

His eyes widen.

"You—poisoned—me—bitch," David forces out.

"I do love our little pet names." Miranda runs her hand up and down the ax handle suggestively. "But that's not quite right."

David grabs at the tile, tries to drag himself toward his wife, but the floor is slick with fluids, and his muscles are tired.

"Not poison. Just a new kind of meat. Something you haven't had before."

David glances at the ax head. It's already spattered with something fading red to brown. Old blood. *How old?*

"I lied earlier. Peter's been here the whole time."

She throws her head back and screams laughter at the ceiling.

David's mind whirls. Friend's house—project... Except Peter doesn't have friends.

And he never *ever* works.

He glances from the stained blade to the chunks of re-gurgitated meat. There's so much of it. Could it be...

No.

Black closes in. Vision tunnels. Dizzy. And the cold tile feels good against his skin. *Yes, take me. Take me.*

SLAP.

David's cheek stings, and the pain forces his eyes open. Wretched clarity floods in.

"Stay awake, sweetheart. I need you to feel this," Miranda says.

David struggles to move his lips. "W—why?"

"Why? *WHY?* You two swinging cocks ordering me around here like a goddamn chambermaid not enough reason for you? Okay, fine. Let me ask you a question. Do you ever even think about her?" Miranda's eyes are wide and bright and sharp as knives.

"W—who?"

"Your ex, asshole. The one whose skull you caved in. The one you sunk to the bottom of goddamn Lake Travis. *HER.*"

David opens his mouth, but no words come out. How did she find out?

"Was I next? How long would you have waited?" Miranda cocks her head to the side, her eyes searching.

Another blast of pain rocks his stomach, and he curls himself into a tight ball. Something slithers up his throat, plugs his airway, and he gags. Then it's in his mouth and over his lips. A clump of loose, gray meat fiber crawls, bunching and elongating like an inchworm out of his mouth and onto the tile.

"Jesus Christ," David says.

"Wrong again," says Miranda.

David expects her to finish him off with the ax, but she doesn't. Instead, she mutters something in another language, quietly at first, a kind of chant, and repeats it, faster, louder, over and over. The lights dim and flicker.

Now all the meat is moving.

David tries to push himself up, but his arms are dead, useless. The pain in his gut flares, and he flops onto his back. The meat struggles beneath him, inching across the tile floor. It's coming together, gathering into a single pile.

"Have fun, boys," Miranda says and taps the ax blade on the floor. Then she's out of the room, the door swinging shut behind her.

David barely notices. He's too busy watching these strings and globs of wet, partially digested meat pile and wriggle together—and there's *so much*—first it's a few inches high, then it's a foot. *Literally*, a foot formed from undulating slugs of boiled, slick flesh.

David tries to crawl away. Another foot, then legs, standing, writhing, weaved together like living wicker. A pelvis. A minuscule penis. Torso. Arms. Smacking. Sliding. Sticking. Dripping. David's nose crinkles at the damp, putrid stench.

When the last hunk of gristle slides into place, he sees it.

Peter.

Meat-Peter's mouth drops open.

"Dad?" The voice is buried under frothing liquid, but it's him. "What's happening to me?"

He takes a wobbling step forward.

"You—you ate me?"

"I didn't know!" David wants to close his eyes, but he can't. He's transfixed.

"You *ATE ME?*" Viscous orange juices fly from the meat boy's mouth and spatter David's face, crawling down like syrupy tears.

The thing stumbles forward, a gelatinous marionette, compressing and expanding, barely holding together.

"I didn't know!" David repeats. It's all he can think to say.

"Dad, it *hurts!*" Meat-Peter looks at his arms, the backs of his hands, and lets out a wet, gargling screech.

Then the boy falls on top of David with a snare-drum *SLAP*, and there are crawling, slick fingers at his throat, clawing, finding, gripping, squeezing. They're so strong. David slaps at the thing with useless arms.

It screams in his face, "YOU ATE ME," over and over, a skipping record repeating the same two-second clip until it's all he can hear. The words hang in front of him, dripping yellow bile onto his face, breath stinking of death, of decay, of carrion.

With a last pathetic twitch, he sinks into black.

⌁

Miranda peeks in when everything goes quiet. The magic only lasts so long.

David's on the floor, mouth frozen open, eyes bulging with popped blood vessels. He is covered in a heaping pile of soggy meat and vomit that was Peter again long enough to fulfill its purpose. The boy's gone back to the fire, now, and this is all that's left. But meat's all that's left of any of us, in the end.

Serves them right.

Miranda hefts the ax and steps into the bathroom. There's a lot of cleaning to do. If she's learned one thing from her husband, it's that bodies don't just dispose of themselves.

Brandon Applegate lives and writes in a parched suburban hellscape near Austin, Texas, with his wife and two daughters who have so far failed to eat him. His debut collection, Those We Left Behind: And Other Sacrifices is available now on Amazon and bapplegate.com. More work appears in Shredded (Cursed Morsels Press), Theater Phantasmagoria (Night Terror Novels), and Dark Recesses Press. He is the EIC at Hungry Shadow Press, where he edits whatever weird anthologies he can think of.

If I carry you

Emma E. Murray

IF I CARRY YOU

EMMA E. MURRAY

A DRIZZLE COLLECTS on the window and runs down the glass while the doctor speaks. I'm holding Katie's hand. Tubes and wires snake around her, burrow beneath skin. Her chest rises and falls with the rhythm of deep sleep.

"We'll set everything up with hospice. They'll make her comfortable. All you have to do is love on her."

"Okay," I say, but I don't feel the words on my lips. My entire body goes numb.

Katie snores a little in her sleep. The sheets crinkle as she stirs. The doctor tries to put his hand on my shoulder, but I slip away. Sweat beads across her brow and upper lip. With an edge of the sheet, I wipe it away. Inside me is nothing. I curl my toes, trying to clench the floor through my shoes, feeling that if I don't, I might float away.

It's nice back at home without the injections and tubes shackling her to the bed. Her freckles come back with afternoons in the backyard. She giggles and plays like a child of nearly four should. Her smile returns, but always thin, always tentative. Like she knows.

Then one morning, a new pain creeps in. The nurse

gives her something, but she still rubs at her belly and chest.

"Momma, it hurts."

"I know. I'm sorry." I hold her close to my chest, tears soaking through my shirt. "I'd take it away if I could."

The good days fade and we huddle together under sheets, sleeping when we can. I don't understand how a child so little can handle so much.

I watch Katie sleep. The nurse sets her hand on my arm and takes a breath, holds it a moment. I know what she wants to tell me.

"No, don't."

The words float between us, stark and bare, something unspeakable. She nods, her face pinched, starts the drip and leaves. I curl up on the bed next to Katie and watch her chest rise and fall. I watch her all night, and before the dawn is more than a hint of pinkish gray, I feel her begin to winnow away.

My fingers scrabble for her hand, clench it too tightly, but her eyelids merely flutter as she drifts back into sleep.

"No. Please," I whisper. She answers with a sputtering cough that still does not wake her.

The minutes stretch into hours. Her teeth clatter together, a soft sound like dice in a velvet bag, her lips tinged blue. I pull the quilt around her, rubbing her to keep her warm, begging her to stay.

"I can't do it, Katie. You can't leave me."

My heart splinters, the shards piercing through me. I have to do something. A spark of electric blue bolts across my field of vision, the anguish so intense it's visible.

Her last breath approaches. It circles us. I can feel it with every part of me that had once lived just to grow her, make her whole. And then something in me is changing. A drastic change is necessary, and my body acquiesces.

A shiver crawls through my mesentery, ripples into muscle and the marrow of bones. I feel myself opening.

My ribcage expands, tearing skin with the quiet rip of cloth pulled apart, the threads torn from each other in unwoven ragged edges. There is a faraway pain, but my love eclipses it. I can save her.

She whimpers, pleading like a puppy who's not yet opened her eyes. My torso has fully opened, and there's an excruciating cold as my organs beat and writhe, exposed. I take Katie in my arms, setting her against my pounding heart. My ribcage embraces her as I tuck her limp limbs in, curl her up so small as to fit inside me again. There's a shift and stretching as my organs make room around her, sticky sliding as they rearrange around her delicate face. My hips unhinge as my body morphs to create a perch for her. She nuzzles against my liver. Her fingers reach up and graze my spleen. Her eyelashes flicker in butterfly kisses against my ballooning lungs. I look down, hold her, and feel a tiny sigh, but it's not her last breath. She's relaxing, falling asleep within me, like she did all those years ago.

I close around her. She still threatens to slip away, but I won't let her. My veins and arteries slither into her and bring her oxygen. My stomach melds against her to share our sustenance. As my body fully encases her, I dream of a new placenta growing beside her—an organ specifically to maintain her homeostasis, her life.

I feel her mouth working from within, full of blood, but I know what she's saying. She forms the words, "Thank you, Momma." A sob flows through me and I trace my fingers across my swollen belly, the seam of thick scar tissue already growing to tie me together again.

On trembling legs, I push myself off the edge of the bed and stand. The familiar aches and heaviness of pregnancy overwhelm me, but there's a smile on my lips when I pat my belly, feel the movement within as she settles against my spine, stroking me back through layers of muscle and flesh.

I cradle her inside myself and on buckling knees, carry

the child within myself, never to let her go again until my body fails, whether that be years, days, or hours. I can't tell, but the pain makes me think we have less time than I'd hoped.

At least I won't have to live a second without her. When I die, she'll continue on for minutes, maybe longer, warm and protected. Then we'll leave this place forever. I'll never have to lose her. Never have to say goodbye.

I pad across the floor on already swelling feet, my hands under my bulging stomach.

Reaching down, I touch the skin between us. I hum a little, feeling my face dewy. Glowing.

I'll carry you, Katie. Don't worry. I will carry you.

Emma E. Murray (she/her) writes horror and dark speculative fiction. Her stories have appeared/are forthcoming in anthologies like What One Wouldn't Do and Obsolescence, as well as magazines such as Pyre and If There's Anyone Left. When she's not writing, she loves playing pretend with her daughter and being an obnoxious bard in D&D. To read more, you can visit her website Em-maEMurray.com or follow her on Twitter @EMur-rayAuthor

ROWLAND BERCY JR.
DR. PARASITE

DR. PARASITE

ROWLAND BERCY JR.

IRENE'S STOMACH rolled and she felt light-headed and nauseous. Electrical signals traveled from her brain to her diaphragm, and she slumped over as her abdominal muscles contracted, intensifying the pressure within her gastric system. Before long, the meager contents of her stomach rocketed up through her esophagus and spewed forth from her mouth and nose in a torrent. Irene shut her eyes against the pain as the bitter taste of chicken noodle soup and bile splattered to the wooden floorboards.

Eyes blurry with tears brought forth from the vicious expulsion of her lunch, Irene brought her hands to her face to wipe away the mucus dripping from her nose and mouth. She seized what she had assumed to be a few pieces of undigested noodles which exited her nose and deposited on her upper lip then looked down at her hand. Her eyes went wide, and she screamed in disgust at the wriggling mass of pale worms covering her palm. Her screaming intensified, and she crawfished backwards, trying to put as much distance between herself and the spreading puddle of vomit when she looked down and saw that it too was swimming with hundreds of writhing worms. The creatures slithered serpentine through the bile, twisting and sliding and under one another in a wretched pool of disgust and confusion. Her frantic shouting snapped her spouse, Franklin, from his stupor.

Both Franklin and Irene, who had been married for over fifty years, were stripped down to their underwear and fastened to one of the ceiling's support beams by a length of chain. One end of the chain was wrapped and double locked around the beam; the other end snuggly fitted around their necks.

Franklin's eyes went wide with recognition when he noticed a man standing not far away.

"You! I know you. You're that guy from the restaurant. What are you doing? Why are we here?" Franklin asked, panic clear in his voice.

"My name is Jacob. I'm a scientist. I work for a research facility which specializes in the study of various types of Helminths, or parasitic worms. Both you and your wife are part of a trial I'm conducting on host/parasite incubation and evolution. It really is quite fascinating."

"Those," Jacob continued, pointing to the wriggling pile of vomitus in front of Irene, "are your children. It should fill you with pride to know that you have been personally selected by me to play a pivotal role in the study of a new batch of genetically altered, aggressive parasitic roundworms. Two days ago, while at lunch, both you and your wife ingested salad onto which I sprinkled hundreds of eggs, laid by genetically modified female roundworms."

Jacob beamed with pride.

"You're fuckin' crazy," Irene shouted in anger.

"Maybe so, but here we are." Jacob turned to leave the attic. "I'll be back in a couple of days to check on you."

Upon his next visit, Jacob recoiled when he entered the attic. The stench of vomit and feces assaulted his nasal passage. Franklin and Irene were laying in puddles of worm-infested dysentery and bile, both covered in filth and looking shattered. Their bellies were swollen to almost twice their original size. Hundreds of worms swam through the puddles soaking the floor around the couple.

"I'm impressed, it looks like you've both been very busy." He held two empty buckets, passing one to Franklin, and the other to Irene.

"The next time you have to use the restroom or puke please do so into the bucket, unless of course you enjoy wallowing in your own excrement and spew."

"Please," Irene begged. "Please, let us go so we can get medical attention." A chill ran down her spine as Irene felt a tickle in her rectum. "I can feel them squirming inside of me. I feel them in my stomach and in my backside. It's driving me crazy."

Her eyes went wide as she picked herself up from the floor and pulled down her soiled underwear. She made it to the bucket only seconds before she spewed forth a deluge of bloody, worm infested, greasy dysentery from her rectum. Irene gripped the side of the bucket and shivered in disgust at the feel of hundreds of worms as they purged from her bowels. Unable to do anything other than offer comforting words, Franklin hung his head.

When the cramps stopped, Irene was sobbing hysterically. She reached behind her and took hold of a squirmy cluster of worms still dangling from her rectum. It took her a few tries to remove the batch completely, because both the Helminth and Irene's hands were slick with excrement.

Unable to stand the stench any longer, Jacob crinkled his face in disgust and once again left Franklin and Irene to their own devices.

When Jacob next returned to check on his experiment, the rancid stench of sour bile and pungent excrement permeated the air. And judging by the lifeless Franklin, the putrescent aroma of death would soon accompany the miasmatic cacophony of smells which had already saturated the space. Irene was still alive, though barely. The woman seemed to have withdrawn into her own mind in an attempt to escape the incessant wriggling of the thousands of worms inhabiting her body. She was lying on the floor, staring off into space. Her stretched out, hand resting in a pile of stool. A steady stream of unintelligible words babbled from her mouth and from the looks of it she would soon rejoin her husband in the afterlife.

Irene twitched violently, causing Jacob to once again focus his attention on her. The iris of both of her eyes had frosted over and turned milky white. Her sclera was crisscrossed and red with dilated blood vessels, indicating an inflammatory condition known as Ocular Toxocariasis, which occurred when roundworm larvae invade the orbital cavity. Though Jacob knew well the cause of Irene's eye infection, he never had the opportunity to study it before—at least not in humans.

Jacob reached Irene and squatted on his haunches to get a better look at her eyes. He spread apart her eyelids and looked closely at the numerous larvae wriggling and writhing across her pupil.

Irene's hand closed around the pile of worm-riddled feces it was resting in, and she slapped it directly into Jacob's face. The wet smack caught Jacob completely off-guard and sent him sprawling to the floor. He floundered in the horror he had created. With what little strength she had remaining, Irene dragged herself through the offal until she was at Jacob's side. With what strength her withered, 70-something year old hands could muster, the woman started clawing and scratching Jacob's face, doing what little she could in a last-ditch effort to save herself. "You crazy bastard, look at what you did. You killed my Franklin," Irene screeched as she continued her assault on her captor.

Jacob raised his hands above his head trying to shield his face from the woman's raking claws. He blindly shoved his hands in Irene's direction and sent her hurtling into the support beam she was chained to. There was a sickening crunch when the back of her head made contact with the angled edge of the beam. Dazed and feeling weaker by the second, Irene saw through a blur that Jacob was recovering from the initial shock of her unexpected attack. She knew that if he managed to get out of reach of her grasp, she'd have no chance in hell of getting out of this alive. She took advantage of the only weapon at her disposal: the bucket. She flung the bloody contents into his face. Septic, room temperature waste smacking into Jacob's face for a second time in as many minutes sent him into a rage.

Filled with adrenaline, Jacob made it to his feet but couldn't see Irene through the sludge and worms covering his face. He used his already filthy hands to wipe his vision clear, just in time to see Irene. With the assistance of the support beam, she had climbed to her feet, swinging the empty bucket at his head, though admittedly without much force. He instinctively deflected the bucket and punched her in the jaw.

The devastating blow knocked Irene's bottom dentures out of her mouth and sent them sliding across the floor. She careened backwards into the support beam. Her bad hip, in addition to her already weakened condition, and the struggle with Jacob, proved to be too much for her. Irene slowly slid to the ground, back resting against the support beam, as her legs failed her.

"You wretched old bitch!" Jacob fumed as he stalked

towards Irene. The threat in his voice briefly diminished and made almost comical as he slipped on the diarrhea slick floor and nearly went crashing to the ground. In a last act of defiance Irene giggled at seeing Jacob flailing about as he tried to regain his footing. He steadied himself, made it to the beam and stood over Irene.

"So, you think that's pretty funny, huh," Jacob said menacingly. "Well, old lady, I'll give you something to laugh about." With this, Jacob moved around to the back of the support beam. He took hold of a section of the chain which kept Irene fastened in place, and then grabbed another section of the shackle.

When the woman realized what Jacob had in store for her, she weakly lifted both hands to her wrinkled throat and tried to slip them under chain link garrote. Jacob placed his feet at the base of the pillar and leaned back with the entirety of his weight, pulling the restraint taunt across Irene's neck. Irene's eyes went wide with panic as the chain cut off her oxygen supply. The woman frantically tried to pry the improvised noose from around her neck, but she was no match for Jacobs's strength. All efforts to free herself were ineffective. Irene began wheezing and gagging.

"What'd you say?" Jacob grunted as he pulled back harder, applying more pressure to his makeshift strangulation device. He laughed and said, "look who's laughing now, cunt," when he glanced up and saw Irene's feet thrashing about in the air on the opposite side of the pillar. Jacob would have laughed harder if he could have seen Irene's face. The woman's lips were turning blue, and her eyes protruded comically out of their sockets. Jacob kept the chain taunt around her neck and it didn't take long until Irene could do nothing but succumb to her captor's fury.

Her struggling began to subside. Her hands slowly slipped down from the chains wrapped around her neck and twitched at her side. It didn't take long until her already blurry vision converged into a single pinpoint, before blacking out completely as death's cold embrace united her in the afterlife with her sweet, sweet Franklin.

Exhausted and in desperate need of a shower Jacob stood and made his way toward the attic door. "Well, this experiment's a bust," he said aloud to no one in particular. He wrinkled his nose in disgust as he took in the scene before him, dreading the cleanup he knew he'd soon have to face. "Guess it's back to the drawing board," he concluded before exiting the room, shutting the door behind him.

The following morning Jacob was waiting at an intersection in a school zone. A school bus had pulled over and was disembarking a rowdy stream of middle schoolers. After the incident with Franklin and Irene, Jacob had begun to wonder if a younger, healthier subject might be better suited for his experimentation. As the flow of children continued from the vehicle, all but one headed towards the entrance of the building. A young boy, who appeared to be about twelve years old, darted off in what was presumably an attempt to play hooky for the day. Jacob smiled as the light turned green.

If you enjoyed *Dr. Parasite*, watch for the full novella, to be released in 2023.

Rowland Bercy Jr. is the author of Unbortion, recipient of the 2020 American Fiction Awards and finalist in the 2019 International Fiction Awards. He wrote Payback is a Witch and Pre-Thanksgiving Stress Disorder. In addition, he has had short stories published in various collections, including: Baker's Dozen; Battered, Broken Bodies; No

Anesthetic II: An Extreme Horror Anthology; and Exits. Rowland wishes to reside in a world inhabited by multiracial mer-people who derive nutritional fulfillment by consuming copious amounts of sweetened condensed milk straight out of the can. Until such time, he will regrettably continue to live in boring-ass Houston, Texas. When not reading or writing, Rowland enjoys traveling, listening to 80's music, or catching the latest horror flick at the local theater.

CAVITIES

Monica Louzon

CAVITIES

MONICA LOUZON

MY GUMS THROB, but the pain will be worth it. My lips will conceal the price of victory. I have nothing left to give.

The safe-deposit box lies before me on the treasury floor. I kneel, reciting the words to wake it, and the box's five-cavity locking mechanism protrudes toward me.

I empty a stained velvet pouch on the flagstones, scattering five teeth—my last ones, the blood on them still crimson.

The lock twitches, impatient.

Praying that I've finally cracked the box's code, I arrange the teeth in a line: first canine, oldest molar, youngest incisor, second canine, left front tooth.

With a trembling hand, I place the first canine in the rightmost hole. A shadowy film slides over it. I go down the line from right to left, placing a tooth in each cavity until my last tooth slides into the final hole.

Teeth in the lock churn, chewing.

The box pops open.

The shadows inside shape themselves into a mouth, full of teeth—*my* teeth. They gleam and part, revealing another locking mechanism. A tongue-shaped slot yawns at me.

Weeping, I unseal my lips and lift the box.
It seems I still have something left to give.

Monica Louzon (she/her) is a queer Maryland-based writer, translator, and editor. Her words have appeared in Apex Magazine, Curiouser Magazine, Dark Recesses, Paranoid Tree, Shoreline of Infinity, and others. She is Acquiring Editor for The Dread Machine. Follow her on Twitter and Instagram @molo_writes.

LENA NG

BEAUTY IS IN THE EYE
OF THE OTHER

LENA NG

BETHANY LOOKED FORWARD to her first sleepover. Although she had read about them in books like Sweet Valley High, flipped through pictures of girls gossiping in glossy teen magazines, and watched the fun of escaping from serial killers on VHS, she wondered if she was ready. There were supposed to be pillow fights and popcorn and the sounds of girls squealing. There should be R-rated movies and drooling over boys and secrets and revelations. It was a rite of passage, one she eagerly anticipated, though it would be her first night away from her parents.

She was brought home two months ago. Her parents had cooed and cawed on the other side of the glass window and pointed at her, leaving smudges on the surface. They had signed the papers and said they didn't need a box. They put her in the eighth grade, based on her apparent age—her height, the length of her feet, the signs of beginning adolescence, signaled by a slight greasiness of her hair and skin. Her birthday was still up for debate, but they determined August 19, maybe through carbon dating.

Bethany was socially way behind, but she read a lot to

catch up. Her parents, ashamed of her ignorance, bought her all the latest newspapers and other publications, and she carefully studied the trends. Jelly bracelets on both wrists, teased hair with big bangs, rolled up button-down striped shirts. She knew of the latest teen heartthrobs: Johnny Depp from *21 Jump Street*, Bon Jovi from the band, Michael J. Fox from *Family Ties*, though Bethany thought he looked too bony, too unripe for her taste. Fashion icons included Madonna and her beauty mark and crimped, black hair. Her parents nodded their approval; they thought she could fit in. Mostly, though, Bethany was looking forward to making a best friend. Someone who could understand her, someone with whom she could share anything.

Saturday, just after five p.m. when it was starting to get dark, her parents dropped her off at the front door. They had advised against bringing any weapons, but now, standing alone at the door, she wasn't so sure. When the door opened, she demurely greeted the parents of the host, adding a curtsy for good measure. She waited until they invited her inside before she entered.

A girl wearing a baggy top and leg warmers over a pink leotard came to greet her. Ashley gave a sparkly wave. "Hey, Bethany," she said and showed her teeth.

Bethany bared her teeth in return. "Bethany" was the new name her parents had given her, and she was still getting used to it. Her name really couldn't be pronounced, not with these primitive vocal cords at least. You would have to do some in depth cutting and reshaping for the correct sounds to be created. Then there wasn't always a guarantee the patient would survive the procedure. You couldn't underestimate the fragility of human flesh.

Bethany followed Ashley into the basement where six girls sat in a circle. There were no candles or pentagrams, so they would not be performing a séance unless they were waiting until after midnight. She sat in the middle of the circle, but moved to the perimeter when she realized the other girls were staring at her.

Ashley began the first sleepover ritual. They crowded around a brightly colored magazine filled with photos of boys with gelled hair and white grins. Slim boys with large eyes. Muscular boys with square jaws. Boys in tank tops showing curves of tender muscle. Bethany wiped away the strings of drool with the back of her hand. She was getting hungry. Linda, a bookish girl, passed her a bowl of popcorn.

At midnight, Ashley turned off the lights. She pressed "Play" on the VCR. They tucked into their sleeping bags when the credits for *Alien Invader Slumber Party Massacre* started to roll.

The other girls screamed, and Bethany happily screamed with them. It was one of the few socially acceptable times for making such a noise and she wished to take full advantage of it.

When her eyes grew heavy, a pillow slammed at the back of her head. She turned and saw missiles of pillows hurled around the room. Bethany caught the next one aimed at her face with her teeth. She shook it until the feathers started scattering.

"You're so weird," said a girl with wires buttressing her teeth. Her hair was tied in a purple scrunchie. "You're not from around here, are you?"

Bethany didn't know what she did wrong.

There was a distinct chill in the air. They returned to their sleeping bags and stared at the ceiling.

The girl beside her, an athletic specimen named Jessica, rolled over in her sleeping bag and tapped her. "I'm going to the bathroom. Come with me."

Bethany didn't see the point, but if this was part of the experience, she was willing to be open to it. They fumbled their way in the dark, hands groping along the wall for the light switch. She waited outside until Jessica was finished.

After she washed her hands, Jessica opened the bathroom door and waved Bethany to join her. Jessica started to comb her hair, peering into the mirror to examine every bump and splotch. "You're new here. Who's your best friend?"

"I don't have one."

"I'm between best friends too. Judy is best friends with Tiffany, and Carol is best friends with Dawn, and Paula is best friends with both Allie and Frieda. I used to be best friends with Krista, but she ditched me when she started seeing Gary."

Bethany examined the pink gloss that Jessica dabbed on her lips. "What do best friends do?"

"Pretty much share anything."

"Anything?"

Jessica capped the lip gloss and took off one of her bracelets. "See? It's a friendship bracelet. Now you give me one of yours." Bethany did.

Jessica slipped the rubber bracelet over Bethany's wrist. "Your hands are so small. Mine are the size of melons."

Bethany recognized this one: the ritual of disparaging one's corporeal form.

"I hate my thighs," said Jessica. She was tall and had long, blonde hair, and her thighs looked like ordinary, human thighs.

"I hate mine too," Bethany replied.

Jessica wrinkled her face. "I hate my nose."

"Yes, I hate mine too," Bethany echoed. Mirroring was an important technique, one which displayed empathy and social belonging. It was time for a bonding ritual, the last thing on her list.

Jessica and Bethany examined each other.

"I love your eyes," Jessica said, and took a step into Bethany's personal space. "They look orange. Or green? The color looks different in the light. I hate mine. Boring blue." Jessica turned to run a charcoal pencil around her left eye. "I wish we could trade."

Bethany looked deeply into the other girl's eyes. It would be nice to have a change. "Sure." She pinched her fingers together and with a good aim and quick movement, went for it. She held out the milky blue eye for the other girl to examine, the optic nerve dangling like a loose fiber.

Since Jessica looked like she was about to scream, Bethany stuck her fist into Jessica's mouth. She didn't want the other girls to think she was a serial killer. If anything, she was a scientist. Her fingers softened into tentacles which filled the entire space of the oral cavity. Jessica's lone eye bulged. Bethany set the loose eye on the bathroom counter. She pinched her fingers again and plucked out one of her own orange-green eyes. Elongating the back of the blue eye like a grape, Bethany popped the new-to-her eye into her own socket. She felt a wiggle as the optic nerve reattached. She blinked twice. "That's better. Oops, can't leave you hanging."

She popped the remaining eye into Jessica's empty socket. It didn't look right, though. It was a bit squashed, and the iris darkened into red, and it didn't rotate. Bethany wondered if Jessica's vision was through a crimson veil, though she doubted it since she herself still saw in color and not only in blue.

Jessica couldn't say anything around Bethany's fist. Bethany wondered if Jessica had anything else about her body she wanted to trade and if she could help her again. A wash of contentment flowed over her. What a fun night. She was happy she had the quintessential teenage experience. They had pillow fights and popcorn and she joined in the sounds of girls squealing. There were R-rated movies and drooling over boys and secrets and revelations.

But most of all, Bethany was happy she had made a

best friend, someone with whom she could share anything.

Lena Ng shambles around Toronto, Ontario, and is a zombie member of the Horror Writers Association. She has curiosities published in weighty tomes including Amazing Stories and Flame Tree's Asian Ghost Stories and Weird Horror Stories. Under an Autumn Moon is her short story collection.

GOT YOU TOO
DAVID ROYCE

GOT YOU TOO

DAVID ROYCE

DANNY HILDBRETH WAS HALFWAY home when the sky opened up and the rain let loose with a fury. Winds howled, and the deluge buffeted his exposed skin. He put his head down and jogged towards the bus stop with its weak yellow light and dirty plexiglass sides. It wasn't much, but it would protect him from the storm for the most part. He was soaked through by the time he made it to the shelter, water sloughing off him and forming a puddle around his feet. The rain beat down on the roof of the small structure as Danny Hildbreth shook himself like a dog from a bath.

There was another occupant sitting at the far end of the bench inside the meager shelter. The man appeared to be homeless, his head resting against the side of the plexiglass enclosure, eyes closed, mouth slightly open. Danny didn't want to disturb the man's sleep, so he took a seat on the other end of the bench and hugged himself in an attempt to stay warm. He hoped the rain would let up soon so he could go home and take a nice hot shower. The splatter of rainfall echoed through the shelter, a hypnotic rhythm that soon lulled him into a daze. Danny tucked his chin to his chest and felt his eyes getting heavy.

He jerked himself to attention when he felt pressure on his chest. His head swung up and the face of the old man was inches from his own, the man's hand pressed against Danny's chest as if holding him in place. The stench of urine underpinned with rot assaulted his nose and made him gag.

"It got me. It got me good. And now it's got you too." The old man started laughing, his open mouth revealing blackened teeth and purple diseased gums. But it was the man's tongue that made Danny scream. *No, not a tongue,* his mind bellowed. Where the tongue should have been was replaced by something black and thin. It squirmed and slithered inside the mouth cavity on sets of tiny legs on either side of its body. The realization of what it was hit Danny like a punch to the gut. It was a millipede, about six inches long.

The old man's laughter continued as Danny finally found his strength. He shoved the old man away and jumped up as the man fell awkwardly to the ground. The man never stopped laughing. The cackling followed Danny as he ran toward home.

The rain was relentless and showed no signs of easing. His adrenaline drove him forward and, ten minutes later, Danny took the building stairs three at a time to his second-floor apartment. He pulled his keys from his jacket pocket and, after a few shaky failed attempts, managed to unlock the door. He was completely drenched and felt like his lungs were about to burst. He locked the deadbolt behind him and pressed his back against the door as he tried to slow his breathing and get himself together.

Water dripped on the floor but that was okay. He kicked off his shoes and then got undressed, leaving his wet clothes in a pile in front of the door. He walked naked to the bathroom and turned on the hot water in the shower. The old pipes groaned but complied and as he waited for the water to heat up, he looked at himself in the mirror. The dark circles under his eyes were those of someone twice his twenty-six years. *This is why it's called a grind.* He thought, *because it slowly takes away pieces of you.* His whole life up to this point had been a grind. Kicked out of his home at eighteen, he had set out to make his name as a writer. Dreams of being the next Stephen King danced in his head, but the reality was one of rejections and, even worse, invisibility. He had several self-published collections and books online. But each day, as his sales indicated zero dollars, he slowly realized he would have to do something else until his big break came along.

Freelance work was boring, but it did keep him in the bare necessities. Of course, after borrowing money from almost all his friends, they soon parted ways with Danny. So now he was alone, poor, and barely surviving day to day. He rubbed his face as steam started to fill up the bathroom.

Stepping into the shower, he let the water pour over his body. He thought about that old man at the bus stop. *I was probably dreaming. I nodded off, had a nightmare, and over-reacted when I woke up.* Had to be it. Maybe it was his mind's way of seeing the old homeless guy as a reflection of his future self. Whatever it had been, the hot water stinging his tired skin washed the thoughts of the encounter away along with the sweat from his unplanned run.

After drying off, he slipped into his bed, the stress of the last hours slinking into the background as sleep overtook him.

Danny awoke abruptly with a sharp pain in his stomach. He changed positions, hoping to alleviate it, but it sliced through him again, forcing him to sit up. He grabbed his cellphone from the table by his bed. He tapped the screen and the blue display revealed that it was 3:32 a.m.

He pulled the blanket down and turned on the flashlight. Sweeping the light down his body, he nearly dropped it when he saw the place where the pain had originated. There was something just under his flesh. It pushed on his skin and looked like a bulging vein. He slowly reached his free hand until it hovered over the abnormality. With a tentative movement, Danny pressed a finger against the veiny bump. As soon as he made contact, a searing hot pain roared through his abdomen. He screamed out in agony, eyes closed, teeth clenching around his guttural yells.

Fuck! What the hell is happening to me? He tried getting out of bed. As he stood upright, he instantly doubled over with pain. He dropped his phone and crossed both arms around his midsection. He could feel movement against them as he squeezed tighter. *It's alive. OhmygodOhmygod, there's something alive inside of me.*

Stumbling to the bathroom, he flicked on the light and looked in the mirror. *NoNoNoNoNo.* From his neck down were bumps, protrusions, and oddly shaped bulges pulsating under his skin. It looked like his skin was literally crawling, as things were rising, falling, and oozing.

Danny panicked and tried to pinch at the creeping masses, but they deftly and painfully skittered away from his hands, just underneath his skin. He almost fell to the floor. His mind swam, clawing for a solution. On rubbery legs, Danny found his way to the kitchen. He opened drawers, throwing the contents to the floor in a panic.

An intense fresh pain stabbed him like a knife in his right leg. He looked down and saw the snakelike shapes slithering up and down, just underneath the surface. They were larger now. His knee buckled and Danny hit the floor. He reached up and grabbed the countertop with his hand, pulling himself to a wobbly standing position.

It got me. It got me good. And now it's got you too. That's what the old man had said. The old man that smelled of rot with a millipede for a tongue. *I'm not like him. I won't become him, I won't!*

Danny frantically looked around at the clutter. He found what he was looking for. "I will not be like him," he lifted the knife. He didn't have a proper chef's knife or butcher's blade but this paring knife was sharp enough and would do the trick. Hopping over to his tattered sofa, he plopped down and held the knife in front of his eyes, trying to find his courage. Although the pain spreading throughout his body was increasing, he wavered. *I can't do this. I can't just slice myself open*. He lowered the knife.

A pain came so suddenly and brutal from behind his left eye that he instinctively grabbed for it. His vision in that eye blurred and then went dark. He cried out in agony as something borrowed behind his eyelid. He could feel his eyeball moving, being pushed. With a plop, it freed itself from the socket and dangled precariously. He could feel its slickness brushing against his cheek. Something that looked like a giant beetle slithered from the empty space and fell on Danny's lap.

Danny shrieked and without giving it any thought, raised the knife and started cutting. Each slice added to the cacophony of torment sweeping through his body like a tsunami hitting the land. Each cut created an opening for Danny to slide his fingers into, reaching for the slimy bodies within. He squished each one in the palm of his hand before going back in for another, and another, and another after that. They wriggled and squirmed and bit into his muscles, tendons, and organs, but he refused to stop. Even after realizing the amount of blood that covered himself, the sofa, floor, and coffee table, he continued.

He *did* feel better after a while. Whether from his frantic attempts to cut every last one of these things out or from blood loss, he wasn't sure. It didn't really matter to him any longer. For each one he removed there seemed to be three more taking its place. Soon, his other leg, arm, and groin were a breathing crawling mass of bulges. Still, Danny would not give up. When he felt another new pain behind his one good eye, he didn't hesitate. He plunged the knife straight in and pulled the eyeball free. Now blind and going into shock, Danny relented, and his body smacked the floor as he welcomed the dark void.

⊓⊤

"Danny, open up. What the hell you doing in there?" Mrs. Franklin pounded loudly on the door to Apartment 203 but didn't receive an answer. She sighed and took the master key from her pocket. *Goddamn deadbeats. Always making a mess and raising hell at all hours of the night.* She'd dealt with it before, but she usually waited until morning. However, after three phone calls from other residents about the smell coming from the room, she finally relented and went to check it out. *Four thirty in the morning and I'm wide awake because of a smell. I can't wait to sell this pit and retire.*

When she opened the door, she put a hand over mouth to stifle a scream. Wet clothes were in a pile as she stepped in but that's not where the smell was coming from. A body that had once resembled Danny Hildbreth lay naked on the floor, pieces of flesh strewn about, bits of bloody pulp scattered around his prone flesh. Flies swarmed the grisly scene, counting their blessings for this free buffet. Written in blood on the ground above his head were the words, "*It's got you too.*"

⊓⊤

David Royce is from the United States but has been living in Cambodia for the past five years. He is the author of The Things That Happen At Night (a short horror story collection) and Brookhaven (a thirty-six page slasher/comedy set in a retirement home). He is also the host of the YouTube channel, Horror Reads, where you can watch him discussing his latest scary reads. You can purchase his books here: http://www.gumroad.com/droyce.

Family
Dinner
Ruth Anna Evans

FAMILY DINNER

RUTH ANNA EVANS

"I CAN'T," Janette said. It was time to leave for Jordan's parents' house. "You know it's going to be awful. They're going to say something about my weight."

"You're always so sensitive about that," Jordan complained. "And I don't know why you make such a fuss about going to this thing every year." He shoved his arms into his coat. "Go, don't go, it's whatever."

But Jordan was almost shouting. It really mattered to him. She got her coat and the pile of gifts and got in the car, silent and sullen. She would go, but she wouldn't be cheerful about it.

⊤⊤

"Darling!" Jordan's mother swept him into an embrace. Then her eyes fell on Janette. "Hello, dear." The older woman smiled, showing her teeth. It made Janette's spine stiffen. She knew what was behind it. "You're looking nice and plump this year."

A hearty "fuck you" almost slipped out of Janette's mouth, but Jordan reached back and squeezed her hand.

"Nice to see you, Dorothy," Janette managed.

"Indeed," the woman raised an eyebrow. "We always look forward to having you. You might have dressed up a bit for the occasion, though."

Jordan gave Janette's hand a sturdy pull before she could reply, and they continued into the well-appointed two-story decorated in holiday dressings.

"I bet they're doing the marinade in the basement," Jordan said. "Let's head down."

"Oh my God, do we have to?"

"Let's just get this over with. It's like three hours, tops."

"Easy for you to say." But she followed Jordan down the stairs to the brightly lit basement, with its candles and bowls of candy on every surface.

A group of men clustered around the open bathroom door, giving advice.

"The key is the apple cider vinegar; you never put in enough. It really adds that zest." That was Uncle Brad. Uncle Asshole, Janette called him behind his back.

She could hear Jordan's dad grumbling back. "I've added a whole liter of vinegar, how much more do you want?"

"Worcestershire," Jordan piped up next to her, and she felt the sudden and overwhelming urge to throat-punch him. "It's the Worcestershire that really gives the meat a kick." She knew he was trying to fit in with the guys, but she hated that he was playing their game.

"Son!" Jordan's father, Larry, came out from the bathroom, drying his hands on his jeans. "I'm so glad both of you made it!"

He looked at Janette. "You've put on weight, girlie!"

She wanted to sink into the floor. She shouldn't have worn this sweater. She said nothing, but tried to stand up a little straighter and suck in her gut.

"You ready to get in?" Larry asked.

Janette crossed her arms across her chest, shriveling on

the inside at what she knew was coming. Jordan looked at her, his eyes pleading.

"Come on, babe. It won't be that bad. It's a tradition." Jordan softened his voice. "Please?"

Janette's only choices were to throw a hissy fit and leave, or do what they all wanted her to do—what they'd all prepared for her to do. And how often did Jordan say "please"?

Her arms dropped to her sides in defeat.

"Fine, but I'm not taking my clothes off for the marinade."

Larry patted her on the arm in a fatherly way. "Of course not, dear, of course not. The soak is better with the skin covered, anyway."

The marinade took two hours. The liquid penetrated Janette's pores, flavoring her. It stung. Uncle Brad peeked in and giggled. Janette squeezed her eyes shut and tried not to let the fumes from the vinegar get to her, but it was impossible. By the time they pulled her out, her eyes were streaming tears against her will. She always tried not to let them see her cry. She always failed.

They undressed her, peeling her clothes off like she was a soaking wet toddler. She held her arms over her head as they squeezed the damned sweater over her bulges, trying not to fall as they removed her pants, a second skin reeking of vinegar. She stood, naked and shivering, arms across her breasts.

"Never could get that one to shave, could you, Bud," Uncle Brad tousled Jordan's hair. Janette gritted her teeth and dropped a hand to cover herself.

"Here," Dorothy said, holding a bright red apple up to Janette's mouth. "Bite."

Pick. Pick. Pick.

Janette was spread-eagle on the table, naked, white flesh exposed, cellulite and stretch marks on display. Jordan's family dissected her with glee, forks pulling her flesh apart like pork.

"You should've made her get a pedicure, son," Dorothy scolded. "Janette, these toenails really are atrocious. It's putting me off of my appetite."

"I'll take a breast," Uncle Brad guffawed. He grasped a carving knife and removed her left breast like a clumsy surgeon. The blade in her skin hurt, but not as much as the embarrassment when Brad lifted her breast tissue between thumb and forefinger. It jiggled.

"What do ya' say, Jordan, a B-cup?"

Jordan avoided Janette's eyes, which were still streaming.

Uncle Brad laughed obscenely. "Small for her size, but at least it's white meat."

Har har har, Janette thought to herself. *The racist, gross, dumb uncle. What a treat.*

"It's your turn, son," Larry said, handing Jordan the carving knife and a serving fork. Jordan was stationed at Janette's generous thigh, the one he gripped during sex.

"Really, I shouldn't—"

"None of that nonsense, sonny, tell us how you feel!" Larry slapped his son on the back as though to dislodge a stuck piece of meat.

Jordan tentatively poked her thigh, then nodded to himself, smiled, and stuck the fork in with gusto. Clear juices squirted out of her flesh. "I do wish she'd shave her legs once in a while." He sawed with the carving knife, peeling off a healthy serving of meat. "And it would be nice if she could cook a halfway decent meal." He showed off his prize, glistening with fat. "And she really has put on some weight." He laughed with his family now, his chunk of Janette extracted.

She closed her eyes and waited for it to be over.

They stuffed themselves on her, picking her apart to the bone, chewing and laughing and riffing on each other. They pried out her clavicle and let the children break it between them like a wishbone.

"Big boned," one of the aunts said with a shake of her head when it at first refused to snap. Everyone laughed.

"Really son," Dorothy said, leaning back and letting out a small, polite belch. "I wonder why you'd even consider marrying her."

Jordan patted his stomach. "She said yes, so I guess I'm stuck with her now." He gave what remained of Janette's butt a pinch, as though he was sharing this little dig with her as a couple's jest. She writhed away from him, upsetting some glasses.

"Now, now, it's just a joke," Larry said, patting her exposed femur.

"We have Tupperware," Dorothy announced, but the family members all groaned that they couldn't eat another bite and didn't have room in their fridges to take any home.

Janette gave a sigh of relief. Last year, Dorothy had convinced them to take leftovers and she had thought the sawing and gouging would never stop.

⁜

It was time to clear the table for Bingo. Janette and her remaining parts sat up. She spit out the apple and got to her feet, scavenging for as many pieces of herself as were left scattered around on abandoned plates. She was missing most of her toes; despite Dorothy's protests, Janette knew they were her favorite.

She forced herself through the game, then opening

presents, then dessert. One of the teenage cousins popped one of Janette's eyeballs out and crunched on it in lieu of cookies.

"Is it good?" Jordan asked.

"Not sweet enough, kind of salty." The boy made a face but kept chewing.

***

Finally, *finally,* when it was dark outside and Uncle Brad was three sheets to the wind, it was time to go. They gathered their gifts—a mixer and a bar book—and headed to the door. Her clothes hung loose on her bones. Little bits of meat clung to her in bloody chunks under her sweater. Both breasts were gone. Her legs were gristle and bone.

"Thank you so much for coming." Dorothy smiled at Janette, her expression bordering on genuine. "At least you lost a little weight."

"Of course," Janette said, forcing the words through what was left of her mouth. "Thank you for having me."

***

Ruth Anna Evans is a writer of short horror fiction, an anthologizer, and a cover designer who lives in the heart of all that is sinister: the American Midwest. She has been composing prose of all types since childhood but finds something truly delightful in putting her nightmares on the page. She has published the horror collection No One Can Help You: Tales of Lost Children and Other Nightmares, along with novellas, novelettes, and several short stories. Follow Ruth Anna on Twitter @ruthannaevans, on Facebook at Ruth Anna Evans, on Instagram at ruthannaevanshorror, or at her website www.ruthannaevans.com for updates on her work.

PROPER
CONTACT
MAINTENANCE

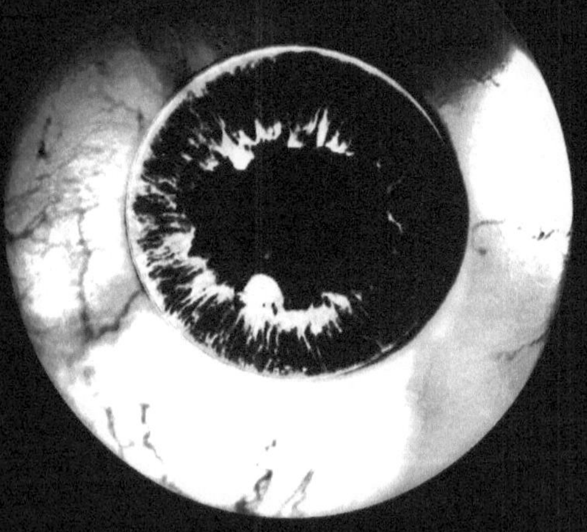

CAT VOLEUR

PROPER CONTACT MAINTENANCE

CAT VOLEUR

"NEVER FALL asleep with your contacts in."

It was the first rule they had given Skylar when she had made the switch from glasses. It had been easy to follow, and so she had.

As she wakes now, however, she can feel the sharp edges of the drying plastic between her lids.

She can't remember taking the lenses out. She can't remember anything from the night before. She's fully dressed beneath the sheets and sporting the cotton-dry mouth of a hangover. Her head pounds as she forces herself to sit. Her eyes feel bruised to the sockets, and it's a struggle to open them.

The world looks cloudy.

Instinct brings her hands to her eyes to wipe away the accumulated webs of mucus. She doesn't make it far. The moment her knuckles touch the corners of her eyes, a searing pain shoots through her head. Her fists trail strings of goo with them as they come away.

The contacts.

It is her first coherent thought, and she knows it's right. She needs to get them out.

The hallway spins as she stumbles along to the

bathroom.

Skylar flips the switch and the lights pierce her like twin irons through her skull. She shuts them off hastily and fumbles in the dark with her contact case.

I just need to get them out.

She is not looking forward to that part, but she tries to focus on what will happen after. Visine. Aspirin. A few bottles of water. Her sleep mask.

She pictures these comforts as she washes her hands thoroughly.

This is another thing she is supposed to do before she handles her contacts — a rule she is not as diligent about. Often she comes home from work, or the bar, late and exhausted.

And how many days did I forget to clean the case?

How often have I used dailies for a week or more?

How many days have I been wearing these?

It feels foolish now, how she prides herself in following one rule, when all the rest are broken.

Never again. She promises. *I'll be better.*

When her hands are clean and dry, she opens her eyes to the darkness as wide as they will go. Starting with her left, she gingerly places the pad of her index finger.

Even the darkness goes red.

Despite barely applying the required pressure, it feels as though she has gone knuckle-deep into her eyeball.

The urge to recoil is strong, but she needs to get the lens out. Her breathing is shaky as she begins to slide her finger down, toward her cheek.

Usually, when she leaves her contacts in too long, they feel thick, easier to grab, eager to come off her eye.

Now it feels as though the damn thing has been plastered down from a night's worth of discharge. She feels a small shift, a sting, and then more resistance. Her finger is tacky as the gooey strings try to stop the separation of the lens from her eye.

Skylar braces herself, her right hand gripping the sink for support. She presses harder and gives a final tug.

There is a cool sense of relief as the lens comes free. It does not feel dried out or sharp now that it's out. It feels more like a gel. It's wet.

She doesn't have time to consider that, dropping it into the sink with a splat as the pain suddenly hits her.

The scream tears through her dry throat before she can think to stop it.

There is an intense, burning pressure that radiates through her entire face. Her left hand is less delicate this time as it begins to scratch at the socket. Her hand is sticky, and when she turns the light back on, she learns that it's also red.

Skylar can only see out of her right side now. She can *feel* in her left side, her heartbeat pulsing in what remains of her mangled eye. The glimpse she catches of the swollen, leaking orb is too much.

Her stomach churns.

She doesn't understand what has happened, what *is* happening.

The rest of the scene is processed only in fleeting images.

The blood dripping down the cheek of her reflection.

The translucent bit of film, twisted around itself in the red pool of her sink.

Her left contact, floating in its saline solution where she had left it the night before.

Cat Voleur is the author of Revenge Arc, and co-host of two podcasts; Slasher Radio and This Horror Life. You can learn more about her and her work from her website catvoleur.com. She can be found on Twitter @Cat_Voleur.

THE
GOD
CARCASS
LOR GISLASON

THE GOD CARCASS

LOR GISLASON

ON A QUIET DAY, above the sea, a slice of heaven ripped open. Small at first, the tear grew, forcing a massive furry lump into our world before vanishing. It fell from the sky with a thunderous clap, a crash that raised the waves and killed the animal instantly. Spat out of dimensions unknown, it collapsed under the weight of Earth's gravity, flesh torn asunder, a masterpiece of creation reduced to detritus.

Thick ichor billowed from burst vessels, the ooze torrenting outwards to the waters beyond. A tangle of limbs, some long and prehensile, some short, thick and bulbous, bobbed on the surface, never to work again. Roiling folds of fur-covered tissue sagged, featureless mounds of flesh save for a single, enormous eye, clouded and lifeless that gazed at the clouds above.

With no islands for miles in each direction, this grand death was witnessed by only the Sun. No one to see the rippling water, changing colors as it cascaded outwards, the thick slime sloughing from the corpse creating a heavy sulphuric tang that carried on sudden winds.

Curious seabirds were the first to approach the goliath, cautious but greedy, eager to feast on creatures both living and dead. A buoyant, easy source of meat was an opportunity too convenient to pass by, regardless of risk. The first to fall taught their comrades the rules of the game. The unlucky gull landed on a soft, flat plateau of skin, where it ripped and tore at the beast until satisfied. Soon it began to shriek in agony, flapping its wings furiously to escape. Webbed feet twisted, fruitlessly, as it was pulled into the rotting carcass with a wet, suctioning noise.

Panicked squawks emanated. Circling like carrion birds, the gulls considered their next move until a powerful *BANG* and a fresh stream of spoiled, frothy discharge erupted from the beast like a burst balloon, then there was a scattering of feathers and the final cries of the flock as they left for less volatile foodstuffs.

Now deflated, the mass finally began to sink beneath the waves. All that remained on the surface was an oil-slick puddle, moss green. As the water settled, the mat began to undulate, expanding.

Marine snow comprised of thousands of particles preluded the beast, a single organism now spreading to the countless depths, the one becoming many. A communion.

Hundreds of fish arrived, summoned by the drifting smells and samplings of blood in the water. They savaged the underbelly, a serrated mess of otherworldly organs spilling forth, releasing more slop.

The frenzy was endless, pieces breaking free and instantly snatched up by schools climbing over each other in desperation. The scent of decay was intoxicating, summoning countless species to partake in a blur of activity. This murmuration of fish orbited the rot, a whirling death cult sucking in anything that ventured too close.

Finally, it reached the sea floor, displacing a whirlwind of sediment and invertebrates. The dome of writhing flesh covered the leviathan, acting as a convulsing barrier. Rays of shimmering light danced through gaps as they constantly shifted. Nothing could hope to breach the chaos as it radiated death and destruction. Scavengers who approached were hurtled away, ripped from the sea floor with a violent fury.

Remarkably, this did not deter every creature. A solitary crab, sensing the mass, approached from a great distance. The stench of rot tinged with bizarre sparks of heat was impossible to ignore, even with the danger of predators. Flashes of light directed the crustacean onwards even as it was pushed back by the currents. Making the journey from the safety of its protective reef hideaway was tedious. It seesawed like this for hours. When tired, it would nibble on bits of flesh that drifted outwards from the dervish. These offered a strange brightness to the crab, a warmth that bound to its shell, sprouting barnacle-like growths that quickly multiplied.

Spurred on by some unseen force, the crab continued even as its body struggled to articulate with the tumors now weighing it down. Cracks began to form in the carapace, spongy tissue spilling through. The eyestalks sagged, drooping like flowers before twisting together to form a helix.

Finally it reached the swarm. The fish who once made up the tornado had ripped their bodies to shreds, the cloud of blood and swirling particles all that remained of a once mighty school. The crab easily passed through this haze. Its legs pierced the sands deeply as it dragged its nodose body towards the eye of the storm.

The carcass from the heavens sat before the crab. Journeying from its world to ours had mangled this once great beast, though still formidable, even as it decomposed at the bottom of the sea. Its fur shone with an unnatural light, refracting off particles in the water. Fore limbs hung down like an enormous set of ribs, with a concave torso visible beyond. The once skyward facing eye, now punctured and weeping fluids, sat in the center of this cavity, perhaps consumed by a hagfish or other predator that broke through.

Pinchers extending, the crab tenderly explored the opening. It grasped a segment and ate the flesh.

This first bite awoke something within the arthropod. A biological need. It followed fresh tunnels into the mass, turning this way and that, occasionally stopping to eat. The warmth it felt had now grown to a persistent burn, pushing the crab onwards.

Finally it breached into an organic chamber, a pocket of air despite the depths. A layer of thick mucus covered the room. Hanging from the ceiling was an opaque egg sack, dripping fluids. A single webbed foot was visible from within, pressed against the taut skin. The inner heat grew to a blazing inferno. Without hesitation, the crab reached for the ovum and began to cut.

$$\pi\top$$

Lor Gislason is a queer autistic author from BC, Canada who loves all things goopy. Their debut novella Inside Out is available from Darklit Press. They are the editor of the upcoming Bound In Flesh: An Anthology of Trans Body Horror with Ghoulish Books. They live with their partner and two cats.

Dan Scamell

Mommy won't wake up right

MOMMY WON'T WAKE UP RIGHT

DAN SCAMELL

THE VIOLENT BUZZ of my phone vibrating against the fake, composite-wood top of my bedside table wrenches me out of a deep sleep. Following the initial shock of that hateful buzzing, a ringtone plays. It's the chorus from, *Hip to be Square* by Huey Lewis and The News, the ringtone I've assigned to the phone I gave my daughter. I tap the screen to answer before Huey even gets the chance to say, "square" and speak urgently, but groggily.

"Brenda? Izzat you?" I practically shout into the glowing rectangle. There is silence at first, "Brenda? Sweetheart? You there?"

"Daddy . . .?" she croaks, barely louder than a whisper.

"Yes, I'm here. Talk to me mugwump, are you okay?"

"Daddy, it's Mom. I think she's sick."

"What's the matter with her? Are *you* okay?" I'm already sitting up, pulling on sweatpants. I look at the clock hanging on my wall, It's 4:10 a.m.

"I don't know." She pauses for a long time before saying, "She's . . . sick." It sounds like she's been crying and is about to start again any second.

"Okay honey, just hang in there, I'm going to head over

and check on you. Just sit tight in your room, okay? I'm coming over right now. You hear me?"

"Yeah," she breathes. "I'm scared."

"It'll be okay. What's wrong with your mother? What does she say? Can she talk?"

"She looks funny. Her eyes are open big but she's acting like she's sleeping. She looks . . . wet."

Wet? I think to myself. I'm thinking that I know what's going on here now. This isn't the first time Cybil has been "sick" late at night.

"Did Mommy go out tonight?" I ask, grabbing my car keys off the table.

"I think so. I'm scared. She won't wake up right." She's hiccupping sobs now.

"Don't worry sweetheart." I've got on a pair of slippers and I'm leaving the front door, heading to the car. "It sounds like Mommy got dr—made herself . . . *sick* again. She probably just needs to sleep, but I'll be over as soon as I can."

"Thank you, Daddy. Please come soon."

"Just go sit in your room. Try to get to sleep if you can, and I'll be there in fifteen minutes, okay?"

"Okay."

She hangs up.

⊓⊤

By the time I get on the road, most of the fear I initially felt hearing Brenda's voice is replaced with anger and frustration. *Mommy won't wake up right.* She looks *wet*. Cybil probably went out to some bar and got herself all fucked up drinking on her meds again. Most likely she's passed out and sweating through her sheets, maybe she even pissed the bed this time.

I'm turning down the street toward the house where I used to live—where I pick up Brenda every other week-end. I have to try to appeal that ruling again; this is ridiculous.

I ease onto the side of the street and put the car in park. The first birds have started singing, though the sun hasn't risen yet. I open the door with a key that Cybil doesn't know I have, and as I expected, the chain isn't hooked. It's dark in the living room, but before I can reach for the light switch, tiny footsteps come stampeding down the stairs and suddenly there is a little girl here, her arms wrapped around my legs.

"Brenda, honey," I say, trying to sound soothing. I'm rattled.

"Please come look at Mommy, she's being weird, and I didn't know what to do."

"It's okay, you did the right thing calling me. What is she doing that's *weird?*" Some of the rage reverts back to worry again.

"She," Brenda starts, "she started making noises…like —like the noise it makes when you gargle the toothpaste water."

That doesn't sound good. Brenda won't unlock her arms from around my knees, so I reach down and pick her up. She buries her soft, pink face into my neck. I can feel her hot, clammy cheeks on my skin. Holding her tightly in both arms, I climb the stairs two at a time, pace down the hall and turn into the doorway of my old bedroom.

I set my daughter down again and tell her to go to her room and wait for me there. She doesn't go at first, then slowly backs from the room and out of sight. After listening for a moment I hear her bedroom door close. While listening, I notice that I don't hear the gargling noises Brenda mentioned. That's either a good thing, or a *very* bad thing.

I stamp rather loudly over to the bed, ready to turn Cybil on her side and shake her until she wakes up. Maybe I'll even throw in a few slaps to the face like they do in old movies. Looking down, I see what Brenda meant about mommy being "wet." Cybil is lying on her back, gazing blankly up at the ceiling. Her face looks puffy, damp, and sticky. Looking at the sheets and the pillow, I can see that some of her sweat has seeped into the fabric. But something's off. I don't think this is sweat. I thought it had to be at first, but it looks thicker, more oily than sweat ought to look.

In a pang of panic, I pull the covers off of her so I can roll her onto her side. The top sheet is heavy with yellowish oil, and some strings of it stretch several inches from the fabric to her skin before thinning and breaking.

"Cybil!" I shout. "Cybil, wake up!"

There is no response. I turn up my palms and start to slide them underneath her, one at her shoulder and another under her thigh. She's warm and her skin is slick. I lift to start rolling her and I feel my fingers sink into the meat of her body. Before I can even fully register that this is not a normal sensation, my right hand slips and shoots up through what used to be her thigh. It's passed entirely through her leg with barely any resistance. I remove the hand under her shoulder and her body jostles back into a lying position with a jiggle.

As she comes to rest again, her head lolls to the right, and her nose and lips slide down the side of her face. One of the eyes that was locked open is now covered with the remains of skin and eyelids, and her ear is slowly oozing down the back of her head. Similarly, the flesh on her torso succumbs to gravity and starts receding into the bed. One of her breasts slips downward and smacks against the wet bedsheets.

"Cybil! . . . Christ, Cybil! Cybil!" My brain seems unable to come up with any response beyond repeating her name. I'm about to put my hand over my mouth to help silence the shouts, but stop, noticing that the palm and fingers are coated with a rosy, yellow paste from where I touched her. The viscous slush covers my hand, and threads of warm slime hang and sway from how badly I'm now shaking.

Unable to think of anything else to do, I reach my soiled fingers into my pocket and pull out my phone. I have no idea what 911 could possibly do about this, but I'm out of ideas and on the brink of losing it. I hold the phone in my right palm, and go to punch the numbers with my left, but my hands are oily and slick with the remains of my ex-wife, and the phone leaps from my grasp. The device falls into Cybil's melted stomach with a nauseating plop. In seconds it's completely submerged.

The woman's body flattens and seeps toward the edges of the queen-sized bed—a mound of soft taffy, virtually unidentifiable as human. Gagging back terrified sobs, I feel hot tears prickle around my eyes.

"Daddy…" says a tiny voice from the hall.

"Brenda, no!" I turn and see her in the doorway. "Don't come in here. Just…Daddy will be there soon, just go back to your room and…" I trail off. Looking at her I can tell she's scared to death, and I can't blame her. I am too. Her face is puffed up and glistening with tears. I walk forward to try to block the remains of her mother from her view.

"Daddy…I don't—I don't…" she squeaks. I can't stand seeing her so upset.

"Don't worry, mugwump. It's going to be okay; everything is going to be fine." As an afterthought, I add, "No reason to cry, honey. It's going to be all right. Don't cry."

"Daddy…" she says, her cheeks shiny. "I'm not crying."

Dan Scamell is a writer of weird and speculative fiction which takes place in a slightly less pleasant version of the world in which we live. His fiction has appeared in The Molotov Cocktail and is featured in the From the Dead

Anthology 2022. In 2023, his speculative literary novel *Walnut Ridge* is set to be published by Dead Star Press, and he also plans to release his weird erotic novella, *Stuck Together With You*, co-written by V.D. Mercer. He currently lives in Pennsylvania, USA, where, in addition to writing, he creates artwork and watches too much professional wrestling. DVSFiction.com

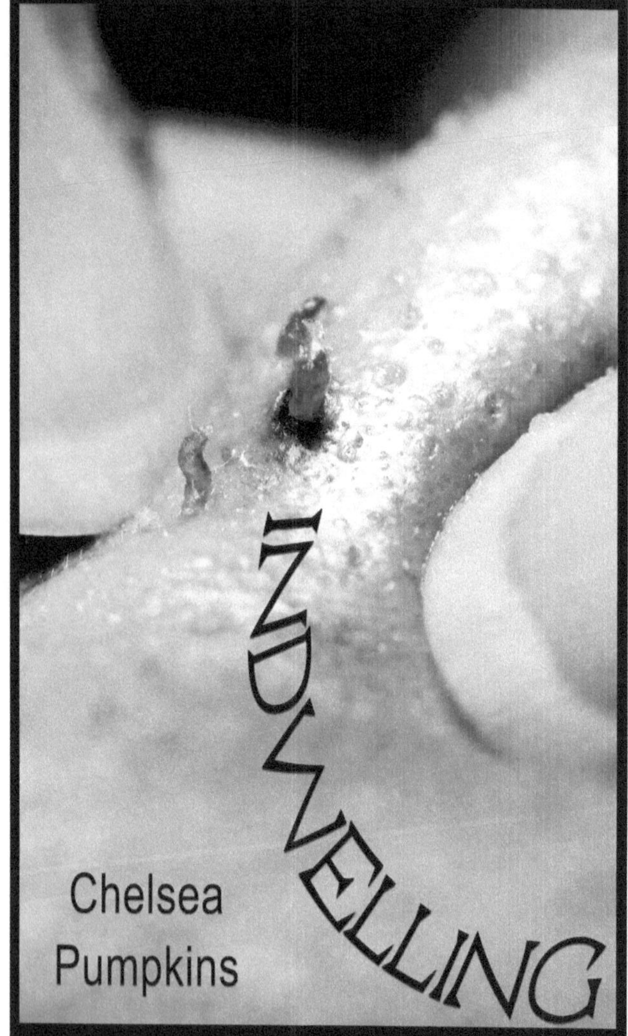

INDWELLING
Chelsea
Pumpkins

INDWELLING

CHELSEA PUMPKINS

TOWARDS THE END, Grandpa forgot who I was to him. He'd squint and scowl and ask me what I was doing in his house. Auntie would remind him—"Dad, that's Ginny. Your *granddaughter*"—but his skepticism would scarcely lift.

"There's poison under your skin," he'd say to me. Auntie would rush to quiet his babblings again, pretending—hoping—he didn't mean what he was saying. But when she'd disappear, he'd meet my gaze with murky eyes and sharp intent.

"I seen it before, you know."

"What's that?" I'd ask.

"The poison." He'd point his gnarled finger at me. "You're blighted. An infestation."

I'd stare back, hardening in silence, swallowing the cold stone of shame.

My family said it was the dementia. I thought it more likely that in my face he recognized the features of my mother. My dull brown eyes, my crooked nose—features of the woman he implored my dad not to marry. The marriage was a rotten fruit on his family tree, and I, the *infestation.*

Lately, I wonder if there was truth burrowed in Grandpa's madness. When I stare at my reflection long enough in the piss-yellow light of my apartment bathroom, I see the poison too.

It has collected and coagulated into tiny white-capped mountains in a range starting at my forehead, trailing around my eyes and down my cheeks. They throb under close inspection, pulsing in time. Pockmarks have formed routes between their peaks, and I swear the paths wriggle. There's no smoothness to my face, no purity, and it disgusts me. I spit at the ugly woman in the mirror. My saliva trails down her face like tears.

"Good," I whisper.

I pour three fingers of bourbon into a rocks glass. The cracking split of ice warms me before I've even had a taste. I pair the drink with kettle chips and settle onto the couch with my laptop. An hour passes while I watch videos of "popaholics" popping zits.

Some have specialized extractor tools; others use toothpicks and butter knives. Whiteheads erupt like volcanoes, spurting white magma across greasy skin in ultra-high definition. Blackheads bulge against pressure until their dark seeds protrude slowly, slowly, then leap from their crater.

Lightheaded from the booze, I sidle up to the bathroom mirror again with tweezers and alcohol swabs. The pimples are redder now, angry. I start with the biggest one, the kingpin to the left of my nose. I press my index fingers to either side and pinch. The mountaintop swells, pressure building beneath the surface.

I push harder.

Release.

Pus springs out like silly string, coiling upon itself in a mound atop my tender skin. I press and press and press until drops of blood appear.

I've cleared the poison.

I clean the pus away with an alcohol wipe, and when I

look down it moves. I squeeze my eyes tight to quiet my quickening heartbeat.

I look again, closer. There is no collection of pus, but a body—slender, sliming, milk-curdled white—writhing against the sting of isopropyl. With doubting hands, I fold the wipe onto itself. A fatal crunch between my fingers makes me shiver. I throw the wipe away.

There's poison under your skin.

In disbelieving defiance, I approach another blemish. At the precipice of my hairline, the whitehead bulges between my fingernails and explodes in a thick creamy stream. Again, the contamination is alive.

I leave it be and watch as it squirms against my skin. It unravels from its coil and its head searches the air like a bloodhound. Deciding on a direction, it bolts across my forehead in an S-pattern and dives into a gaping open pore near my temple. It slurps back under my skin like a spaghetti-o, and its wriggling form scurries away towards my chin before diving beneath.

The heat of bourbon slithers back up my throat, and bile stings with sour menace. I swallow it back boldly. I scramble through my drawer for the magnifying mirror. Holding it to my face, I'm beguiled by the pulsations of thin, long slithering forms beneath my skin. Their movements imperceptible to the common glance, up close I see they've come to inhabit my entire face. They slip, twist, and twitch against one another, knot and unknot themselves, all against the taut layer of my epidermis.

Blighted.

And I can't stop myself. I burst the pimples one by one, expelling vermicelli worms and watching in wonder as they search for another hole to burrow into. My nerves shudder each time they irrupt back into my skin; my face streaked with the wet slime trailing from their bodies.

My eye twitches. A skinny white worm peers from my bottom eyelid and darts across the surface of my eyeball. It wriggles into the corner of my eye, and I follow its path across the bridge of my nose and up my forehead. My lips curl over my teeth as I realize the worms are a part of me. Always have been. Maybe not a poison, but a power.

An infestation.

Not to be exterminated but cultivated.

I find the last untouched pimple on my face and squeeze until it bursts. I delicately peel the worm from my cheek with tweezers. I open my mouth and place the worm on my tongue. The taste of salt and blood spreads beneath its coiled form. It squirms toward my throat, and I help it along. I close my mouth and swallow.

The surface of my neck quivers and the tremble crawls up over my jaw and into my face. One by one, the empty crevices become occupied again. Tiny white dots refill my pores as the clew of worms settles back into its lair.

I paw at the mirror, at the streak of spit across my reflection. It smears and smudges, but I rub until it's clean. I place my hands on the glass, framing my face between them. There's a sparkle in my eyes now.

"An infestation," I whisper, with a smile.

⊓⊤

Chelsea Pumpkins is a writer from Massachusetts. If she's not reading, writing, or watching something spooky, you may find her hiking in the White Mountains with her husband and sweet pitbull, Moose. You can read her stories in the Strangehouse anthology, Chromophobia, and the Sliced Up Press anthology, Bloodless. She is also the editor of the upcoming anthology, AHH! That's What I Call Horror. Learn more about her work at chelseapumpkins.com and follow her on Twitter and Instagram at @ChelseaPumpkins.

AMANDA M.
BLAKE
Dissolution

DISSOLUTION

AMANDA M. BLAKE

THE HUSBAND and wife are all smiles with champagne glasses in their tended hands, but they circulate on separate sides of the party, taste the salt of the sea air in different sections of the house. No one notices, because their needs are met, and other gossip entertains them just as much as the string quartet or the pianist in the parlor.

Nothing about the stranger who weaves among them is immediately notable except that he's attired for the sea rather than a seaside party—practical, worn clothing rather than clothing worn for one night, dull flannel instead of glimmer and shine in artificial light. The evening is warm, so his isn't the only sweat-beaded forehead. But rather than flushed, his sun-leathered skin is pasty, pale, lips and veins blue as though cold instead of feverish. As he searches through the carefree crowd, more and more whispers turn to the subject of the stranger. *Is he sick?* they wonder. *A vagrant begging for alms, a worker seeking better compensation?*

Separated as they are, it takes the stranger and swirl of rumor in his wake to bring the hosts together on the terrace. The wife wears sequins and the husband wears pinstripes. Her shoes raise her above him; her gold jewelry clashes with his silver understatements.

The husband keeps his words friendly but tone icy. "You need to leave, friend. Take a canapé or two, and a flute of champagne, with my blessing. But you can't stay."

The wife makes no effort to pretend at politeness. "You don't belong here. You weren't invited. And you're scaring our guests."

The man raises his gaze, eyes red-rimmed with colorless irises, emptiness behind lifelessness. "But I was invited. The lighthouse called me home when I was left for dead. You were too busy shouting to the wind to notice smoke billowing from the hatch. Then you brought your whiskey into an uncrowded lifeboat and left behind the stranded to what dragged us below."

The man dismisses all attempts by the servants to provide a free meal or politely escort him from the premises. He grabs his hosts by their wrists, his slippery, clammy palms smearing thick sweat on their skin, drawing them closer to each other than they'd been in almost a year.

"Such things I have seen that man's bald eyes were never meant to see. Drowning nightmares and bubble screams, tentacles to the very depths and a trench-empty stare, salted brine and bloat that I did nothing to deserve. But you..."

Both husband and wife wrench away, repulsed disgust drawing ugly frowns down their faces.

The man doesn't finish his thought, whether caution, accusation, or threat. Thin-lipped, he stiffly turns, leaving splashes on the tile as he allows himself to be removed from the party, to walk the beach, into the tide, and back into the sea, for all the guests or their hosts know. He enlivens conversation about the place of laborers and the appropriate venue for social grievances but doesn't dampen the mood or slow the flow of spirits down already inebriated and life-drunk throats.

The beachfront home judders silent, the hosts returning to separate bedrooms on either side of the property, with the same ocean view through open, sheer-draped windows.

Serene, salty morning air shatters with a scream.

The wife bursts into the husband's suite, because although they cannot remove themselves far enough away from each other, no one else has seen them through childbirth and gambling debts, through flu and fussiness, the ugly, messy quagmire of partnership that isn't really the worst of each other. So she runs to him, and he doesn't shout at her to leave him and his hangover in bloody peace, though he pulls the rope to the four-poster curtains to shield himself from the sunlight flooding the room.

She reaches out, arms bare in her breezy, sleeveless nightgown. The prominent veins in her hands tell the beginning of the tale, and he follows the darkened blue lines up the slender length, paler than the night before. Moisture coats her in a fine layer like lacquer on tinted porcelain and plasters the fine curls at her hairline against her forehead, her temple, her neck, which pulses a rhythm dissonant to what vibrates the bodice of her nightgown, as though something moves on its own against the blood flow.

As the husband sits up against his pillows, he notices his cold-soaked bedclothes. When he lifts his arms, he, too, is mapped with darker blood, bruises in the crooks of his elbows. He brushes the vining lines, grimaces from the thicker texture of the sweat on his skin, like jelly residue instead of ocean spray.

He swallows against a shudder of atavistic revulsion. "It's nothing."

"Nothing? It was the vagrant. He was *sick*. And now we're sick." With a shiver of her own, she rubs her arms on her nightgown.

Disquiet tightens its fist over the husband's chest at the darkened smear on the fabric, like oil on concrete. "It's just a hangover. Jump in the pool or the sea. Take a goddamn shower. I don't need your hysterical hypochondria pounding against my migraine right now."

"You're useless. I don't know why I bother." Before she leaves, she glances over her shoulder. "Have another drink."

"I don't have to tell you," he mutters when she's no longer there with the last word.

The next morning finds him in her room instead, a thermometer silencing his protests and her hand on his forehead, but she can't feel anything on him that she doesn't have herself.

The man holds the thermometer from a different angle in hopes that eyesight is to blame. "Ninety-five degrees. Impossible. Too cold."

"Then why do I feel like wax melting in a vat of infernal heat?" The wife drops back on the pillows. "We need to call the doctor. We don't know what the vagrant did to us."

"He just touched us," the man says. "There's nothing a doctor can do. They'll only tell us to rest and drink lots of fluids, then charge us our own limbs for the privilege. All we can do is wait it out."

"How do you wait out hypothermia?"

"A hot bath. You're the one with the tub."

The woman considers, too listless to complain and too strange under her crawling skin to condemn either of them to their usual solitary. "It's not like we've never seen each other naked."

But through shingles, surgery, and skin peels, neither has seen the other quite like this. Sunlight struggles to make something richer of their flesh, but the macerated skin wrinkles and slips, bluish veins darker and more prominent, the miniscule capillaries purple, distinct as bruises. They've soaked through undergarments with what slicks from their pores.

When they step into the steaming tub, a layer sloughs off like paper skin from a bad sunburn, although they're not burned but freezing.

Yet the heat from the bath doesn't touch them. Nothing touches them, except for the overlap of their peeling legs in the subtly stained water, shimmering on the surface and rippling with steady tears as the wife weeps and the husband tries not to let his wife see that he's right there with her.

"Do you remember what the vagrant was talking about, our yacht sinking? Do you remember the lifeboat?" the wife asks, quavering with the water.

The husband shakes his head. They've had many yachts over the years, and between cocktails and straight-up, they've drowned many tragedies. There are many nights, good and bad, that the two of them cannot remember.

ㅠㅜ

The sun is too bright, their joints too stiff. Skin shedding like serpent scales in greater and greater clumps, they send their servants away. Nausea roils like sand in the tide. A constant beat throbs in the back of their minds as day passes into night and they still haven't eaten, can't sleep, barely move, haven't spoken, although she takes the head of the bed and he takes the foot, the bed big enough for both as long as they don't open their mouths.

Morning finds them in the midst of moans, separated though they remain, clothes and bedclothes soaked through—gray in earliest light and nearly blue as the sun rises again. Vascular, mucosal handkerchiefs surround them, a shredded quilt of their own skin covered in shuddering aspic. Their lips are purple, eyes red, veins more prominent now from the overnight shed.

Wheeze in, moan out, no strength in their throats to scream. No hunger or pain, just a blinding glare in hazing eyes. They look to each other and silently wonder:

Why? Why is this happening to them? Why did the man, who they'd never met and hadn't recognized, decide that his infection needed to be shared with the hosts of a party to which he had not been invited?

Why did they deserve this?

Night sinks on their confusion, and their bodies merge in the center of the bed, a puddle of bloody slime like beached jellyfish under the covers, a diffuse awareness in the midst of marital dissolution.

When the maids finally return, for lack of direction of what they should do with the mess, they gather the sheets and toss the slime into the sea, where it sinks and spreads and sighs like relief.

Amanda M. Blake is a cat-loving daydreamer and mid-age goth who loves geekery of all sorts, from superheroes to horror movies, and urban fantasy to unconventional romance. She's the author of such horror titles as Nocturne and Deep Down and the fairy tale mash-up series Thorns.

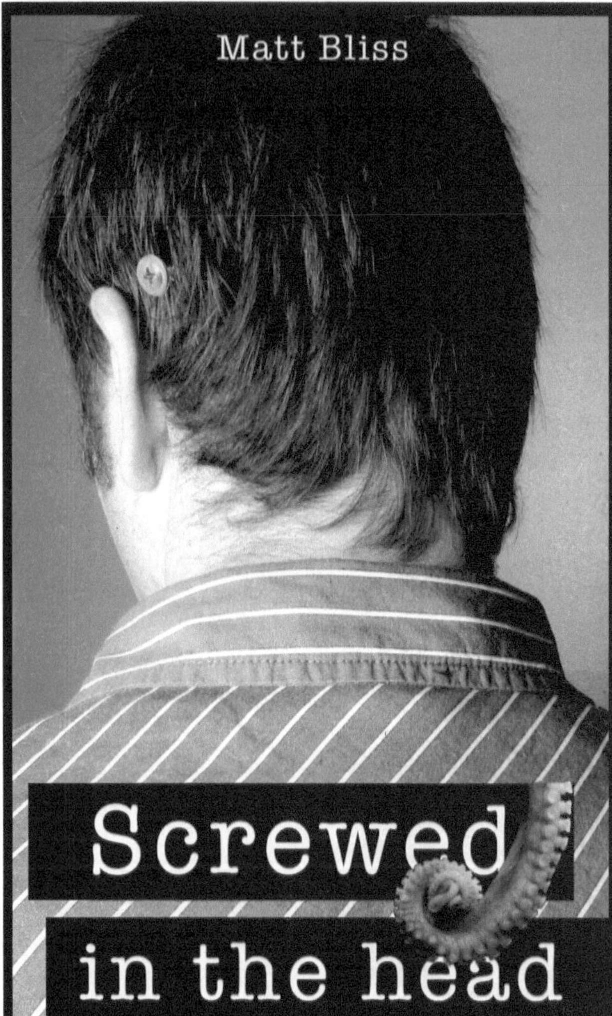

Matt Bliss
Screwed
in the head

SCREWED IN THE HEAD

MATT BLISS

I WAS GETTING a haircut when they found the screw in my head.

The scissors scraped across its metal tip, making a metallic grinding noise that sent electric shocks through my skull right down to my teeth. The hairstylist jumped at the sound, backing away with hands raised high as if the tiny screw was holding her hostage.

I reached up and felt the hard protrusion nestled in my hair: A quarter inch from being flush in my scalp, on the left side of my head, three inches above my ear.

Surely I would have noticed if it had been there before, right?

I tried to pull it out, but it was solid. The threads firmly twisted in tissue and bone. I leaned into my reflection to see it.

Phillips head. Stainless steel.

That evening, I took a screwdriver to it. Placing the tiny cross of its tip in the plus-shaped groove. I squeezed the acrylic grip of the handle and, *lefty-loosey*, gave it a firm twist. My vision went white with pain and my neck jerked back. I torqued harder, feeling my brain underneath, holding to the sinew and threads that keep it in place.

The screw broke free and twisted a quarter turn. I gasped as my vision returned, and it was easy to unscrew after that. Cranking the driver with forearm and wrist as it spoiled out—*one inch... two inches... three inches...* and finally fell free. I held up the mirror and gawked into the hole in my head. At first, only the pink and red I would have expected, but then, something black poured like molasses from the wound.

What I thought was a fluid then came to life. It stretched one ropey black tendril out of the hole and then another. Tentacles quickly took shape, probing the air around me until grasping my arm and pulling itself through the hole. It fell to the floor with a wet slap and wriggled to the darkened corner.

I jumped, panicked, and placed the screw back into its hole. Each turn of the driver was agony, but I twisted it deeper. The tentacles moving at my feet were motivation enough to put it back. I could feel more, too, twisting within my head.

I tried to hide the screw after that—wearing hats or scarves or growing my hair out long—but after enough time, I began to accept it. It became a part of me, the same as an eye or ear or nose, I suppose. A part that I've come to live with, serving a purpose as important as any organ I couldn't spare. So now, I wear the screw with pride.

People often look at it. I catch them when I turn too fast and see the silver gleam of its head in their eyes. They squint and smile and pretend it isn't there, all the while I can read the confusion, *the terror*, on their faces.

They're afraid of it.

Afraid of what's underneath that screw.

Yet some reach out towards it. They want to untwist the screw. To see the horrors that leak out and coil themselves around their feet.

So I let them.

Twitching with a terrified excitement, they turn the screw. The blackened tentacles reach out, slithering their long arms into eyes, and ears, and nostrils. Dark feelers take purchase, growing larger with each dizzying rush of adrenalin. Inside they scream. Inside they laugh. And we all feel alive as they squirm beneath the flesh.

We'll pass one another on the streets much later. They flash a knowing little smile and I will nod in return, because we know what twisting darkness lurks behind our eyes. We can feel it writhing within; waiting for a chance to burst free from the bone and flesh that holds it. And just maybe, one day, they'll reach up and find a screw of their own, just waiting to be loosened.

Matt Bliss is a construction worker turned speculative fiction writer from Las Vegas, Nevada. His short fiction has appeared in Cosmic Horror Monthly, The Nosleep Podcast, and Scare Street's Night Terrors, among other published and forthcoming works. If he's not haunting the used book aisle of your local thrift store, you can always find him on Twitter at @MattJBliss.

Plagued

V.G. Campen

PLAGUED

VG CAMPEN

TAMSIN CROUCHES behind a rose bush and watches the manse across the boulevard. A young soldier in an ill-fitting uniform stands on the front terrace, painting a crude scarlet cross on the double door. The mark of plague. The rest of his troop remain in the street, their faces half-covered by muslin masks. The soldier swipes a final brush stroke and retreats down the stairs, paint pot sloshing red against his trousers.

"*Halt*, damn it," his captain shouts.

The boy stops, though his feet continue to scuffle.

"Set up guard here. If any living soul remains inside the house, keep it inside. And turn away any priest or doctor foolish enough to approach."

Dumbly, the soldier holds out the paint pot, but his mates ignore him. They form a ragged line and march away.

Tamsin retraces her steps to the stableyard behind her master's house, arms clutched tight against her chest. The throbbing in her armpit, she insists to herself, is only the echo of her beating heart, nothing more. She slips into the carriage house.

"Leo? There are soldiers in the street," she says,

fighting to keep her voice level. "They've painted a scarlet cross on the door across the way. Gather your things, we need to leave." This, despite having nowhere to go.

Leo is new to the household, a solemn child who arrived as stable boy a fortnight ago. He reminds Tamsin of the little brothers she left behind. In the harness room she finds Leo sprawled naked on his cot, body lit by weak sunlight strained through dusty windows. A brown-and-white tabby cat purrs at the boy's side, its rounded belly a contrast to the child's shrunken body.

Tamsin steps closer. "Leo?" The boy's fingers are black and curled like claws. Dark purple patches cover his torso, crusted with dried pus and blood. She backs away and crosses herself.

I should cover his body, Tamsin thinks, *do it quickly, just pull the blanket over his remains.*

The cat, indifferent, yawns and jumps to the ground. Tamsin hesitates for a heartbeat, then follows the cat out of the room.

⊓⊤

Inside the kitchen, a lump of incense smolders in a bowl, a feeble charm against the creeping miasma of disease. Tamsin and the tabby cat stand and survey the detritus left by the morning's panicked leave-taking. Master and Mistress fleeing in the coach, taking only the valet and lady's maid with them. Cook and the housemaids slipping away on foot. The room is cool but Tamsin drips with sweat. A sharp pain pierces her armpit, and she can no longer ignore the blue-black swellings that awoke with her that morning. She can no longer ignore the truth. She is plagued and, like Leo, will die alone.

The tabby leaps to the tabletop—forbidden territory for a cat—and struts among the dishes, licking a smear of butter from a plate, sniffing a bowl of over-ripe pears. It jumps to the floor and strolls to the steep back stairway, the servants' pathway to the upper floors. The animal pauses and looks back at Tamsin with green-gold eyes before trotting up the stairs.

Tamsin hesitates for a breath, then follows the cat's trail, climbing two full flights in the silent house and emerging in a broad hall that smells of lemon-oil and beeswax—forbidden territory for kitchen girls and cats alike. Sunlight streams through windows fully three meters high. Fresh flowers sprout from porcelain vases, striped damask covers the walls, thick carpets overlay the floorboards. Pretty things, but Tamsin instinctively recognizes the true marks of wealth: space and light, the absence of dirt, the illusion of a life lived well above the muck.

A slight ticking noise, a rhythmic *pick-pick-pick*, comes from a bedchamber. Tamsin peers inside and sees the cat atop the bed, kneading the satin counterpane, its claws catching and snagging. The tabby has opened a small tear in the satin and Tamsin worms her fingers inside. "They left me here to die," she explains to the cat. She grasps the fabric and slowly rips it open.

Movement across the room catches her attention—her reflection in a cheval glass. *So this is what I look like now.* A reed-thin girl in dirty clothes and apron, face sweaty, eyes rimmed with red. She steps closer. In the hollows of her neck, multiple nodules push upwards, the purpled skin taut and shiny. She'd been pretty once. She knows because men had told her so.

Tamsin unbinds her hair and moves to the washstand, where an ewer of water and a clean flannel await. She wets the cloth and bathes her face, then peels off her apron, dress, and chemise and sloshes water over her body, heedless of the carpet beneath her.

She examines the dark lumps in her armpits, now the size of hen's eggs. Slips her hands along her thighs, between her legs, to find more of the growths, hot and throbbing. She strokes them gently with her fingertips. They are firm to the touch, like ripe summer plums. *The fruit of my loins.* The phrase comes unbidden, remembered from some long-ago Sunday sermon. God may have exhorted Adam to be fruitful and multiply, but Tamsin knows what happens to servant girls who show a belly. They spend precious coin on potions of pennyroyal and wormwood. Visit filthy rooms for unspeakable procedures. Squat in the privy, praying to miscarry in silence.

Searing pain spikes her gut as the first nodule ruptures. Naked, Tamsin collapses on the sodden carpet.

When Tamsin rouses, she is no longer hot, no longer in agony. Her body is slick with blood and pus. She pushes to a sitting position and fragmented shadows skitter away from her, racing across the carpet, swirling like a flock of starlings in the evening sky. The shadows resolve into scores of purple-black spheres which, like a turning tide, now rush back to her. *The fruit of my loins.* They tumble against her thighs, fever-hot. *Flesh of my flesh.*

Tamsin stands and uses the still-damp flannel to dab at the gore on her body. Her hands are clumsy, fingertips a dusky blue-black.

Pounding echoes in the house and a man shouts from the front steps: "Please, may I have water?" Tamsin smiles at the thought of a visitor. She retrieves a full pitcher from the bedside table and, ignoring the servants' narrow stairway, descends the grand staircase. The shadow-dark orbs eddy around her bare feet, cascade like water down the staircase, wait patiently as Tamsin struggles to open the heavy mahogany door.

The young soldier from the manse has ventured across the street. He gapes when Tamsin swings the door wide and reveals her naked self. He turns and stumbles down the stairs.

Tamsin laughs. *A soldier, afraid of me!* She spits into the water pitcher and leaves it on the porch. Perhaps his thirst will force him back.

I will die, but I will die in comfort. She returns to the bedchamber, now redolent with the scent of decaying flowers, and drags clothing from armoires and drawers. Her withered fingers cannot manage the back-laced stays or the buttons and ties of petticoats and hip pads. She settles for shrugging on a brocaded over-gown, the bodice hanging open. When she walks the shadow-orbs trail behind her.

On the window seat, she curls her stiffening legs beneath her as best she can. Across the boulevard, the soldier slumps in his doorway, the water pitcher beside him. The cat leaps to Tamsin's side and begins kneading the folds of her gown, purring mightily. Together they watch the soldier jerk and writhe as the moon rises over the rooftops.

At midnight, the sound of carriage wheels on cobblestones wakes her. The Master's carriage is returning. The coachman walks in the middle of the boulevard, leading the gray horses, the animals plodding like spavined old nags. Tamsin staggers upright and straightens her gown with hands as dry and twisted as old leather. She starts down the stairs to greet her visitors.

The doors in the vestibule bang open. A woman wails about roadblocks and quarantine; a man's voice loudly insists they will find fresh horses and try again tomorrow, search for a road that is unguarded or soldiers who can be bribed.

"The house is cold," the woman cries. "I want fires lit in every room."

Tamsin feels a stab of pity for the poor addled woman, shouting orders no one will obey. "Welcome," Tamsin says from the foot of the stairs. "I am the Mistress of the house now."

The couple hears only a strangled, glutinous heaving. The man raises his lantern; the woman shrieks as light spills over Tamsin.

"Hush now," Tamsin says, as a dark tide of diseased orbs rushes toward her guests. "Be brave. Soon you will be warm enough."

VG Campen lives in a kudzu-infested corner of North Carolina, where she writes by the light of fireflies and swamp gas. Her work has appeared in Pseudopod, Analog, Tales to Terrify, Metaphorosis, and other venues. She is, of course, working on a novel.

BITCH WITCH

BITCH WITCH

PAUL SHELDON

"CHECK THIS OUT." Parker pulled out his phone.

"Oh, you didn't, did you?" His frat buddies gathered round closer, jostling for a look at the tiny screen. "No way!"

"See for yourself. The one and only Emily Rayton, in the flesh."

First his empty dorm room and bed appeared, then Parker walked in with a young woman, lithe, slim, delicate like a model rather than fit like an athlete. She was wearing denim jeans, her long, dark hair vivid against the white of her t-shirt. They kissed passionately for a moment before undressing each other, kissing between each discarded garment. Whistles and crude remarks erupted as the scene unfolded, and more of Emily's pale skin was revealed. Parker fast-forwarded further, put the phone on the table and grabbed a beer. "She's not bad for a library nerd. Enjoy, gents!"

Laughing, swapping high fives and handing out more beers, the group watched the scene unfold. Parker watched for a while, enjoying the attention and the accolades.

"Parker, my man, how many is this now?"

"Our darling Emily is number four."

"Who's next, dude?"

"Maybe we should have a vote. What do you guys think?"

A few names were thrown around, then the group lost interest after promises were made for copies of the latest video to be emailed.

A few minutes later, Mike picked up the phone, frowning.

"Mikey, you better not be staring at my ass," said Parker with mock indignation.

"Dude, have you watched all the way to the end?"

"I was there, man, I'm the star. I don't need to watch the whole thing." The group broke into more laughter, all but Mike.

He handed the phone back to Parker. "Maybe you should."

Parker took the phone. In the video he was lying in bed with his back to the camera, the sheet partially covering his body. Emily rolled over and stood, unashamedly naked, and looked directly into the hidden camera.

"Shit!" Parker gasped. "She knows I was filming her."

Emily shook her head, waved an admonishing finger, and disappeared for a moment before returning. She was holding a small object, difficult to identify in the dim light. She turned, climbed carefully onto the bed, and, without disturbing her lover, slid a hand under the sheet and between his legs. She stood once more in front of the camera, this time empty handed, and blew a kiss.

"What the hell was that shit?" said Mike. The laughing had died down, and the boys crowded around once more to see what the fuss was about.

Parker just stared at the screen, then looked down at his crotch. "That bitch did something to me." He stuck his hand down his pants, then laughed. "Well, everything is still there, boys, I think we're good." Then his face dropped. "There's a hole, a hole underneath my nuts!" He took off, pushing his friends out of the way, and raced into the bathroom.

The doctor appeared to be taking him seriously, but Parker wasn't sure. "I've not seen anything like this before, but I don't think your girlfriend could have done this. It looks more like an infection than a wound."

"You mean she gave me a disease?"

"Highly unlikely, this doesn't look like any STD I'm familiar with. Oh, and there's not just one hole, there are three."

"What?!"

"I'm going to take some swabs and refer you to a specialist, Parker. Let's get this sorted out quickly, whatever it is."

Parker dressed, thanked the doctor and walked out gingerly, thinking of the three little holes in his crotch.

The holes didn't hurt. He was grateful for that as he poked around, using a mirror to find his way. In fact, he could slide a finger into each one, or all three at the same time. They stretched as he pushed, and he could wiggle the finger around inside. It felt weird, his insides sliding over the tips of his fingers, but it wasn't painful and there was no blood.

He called the specialist, made an appointment for the following morning, then decided to skip class and watch last night's football game. He flicked on the television and grabbed a beer, something to take his mind off whatever the hell was happening to him.

The following morning was met with a mild hangover, the sort that announces itself with a dry mouth and a mild thud behind the eyes. Parker got up, went down the hall to the bathroom in his shorts, slid them down, and pissed everywhere but the urinal. From half asleep to fully awake in a heartbeat, he dashed into a cubical.

"Please no," he begged, pulling his shorts down again to reveal a cock peppered with holes, urine still dripping from each one. "No, no, no!"

Shaking, Parker headed back to his room, locking the door. He nervously slid his shorts down and inspected himself.

The holes had spread further and were now all around his crotch and spreading across his stomach. He cringed, a low moan escaping his throat. He ran fingers across the holes at the base of his stomach, just above pubic hair that was falling out in clumps around each hole, leaving his skin with a comical, patchy baldness.

As the tentative fingertips moved across his skin, Parker felt a pleasurable shudder, one that pleased and horrified him in equal measure. He took his fingers away and watched, intently, as his skin pulsed lightly in and out. Placing his fingertips back he felt a breeze with each pulse, as if his skin was breathing through the holes. He held his breath to see if it was his own breathing, but the motion and the flow of air continued, in, out, in, out.

His breath burst out in a gasp, and he slapped his hands over the holes, determined to choke the life out of whatever the hell had invaded him, until he felt the breeze between his legs, and realized he could not cover every hole. He put his hands to his head and screamed.

Parker lay back on his bed and looked at his watch: four hours until the specialist appointment. A lone fly buzzed around the window of his room in a frantic bid for freedom, failing to understand why it couldn't fly through the invisible barrier. Parker couldn't understand what that bitch had done to him. He watched as the fly gave up on the mystery of the window to find another way out of the room, buzzing round and round in an ever-tightening circle, until it landed on his stomach. He swatted it.

The fly disappeared, and Parker sat up. Where the hell had it gone? He felt a tickle inside, under his skin, and heard the unmistakable buzz of insect wings. The fly had gone into one of the holes. He yelped and started squeezing at his skin, pushing and pinching, desperate to get it out. He stopped for a moment to work out where the fly was, but the buzzing had ceased. It had either died or gone too deep to hear.

He grabbed his clothes and got dressed, that damned specialist could see him now, right the fuck now.

Parker tapped his foot impatiently in the waiting room, urging the next name called to be his. The holes still didn't hurt, but he had developed a persistent itch that was spreading ominously and there was still no sign of the fly.

By the time he got in and slipped his pants down on the examination table, holes had spread to his sternum.

"Well, I've never seen anything like this," said the specialist, and that was enough for Parker. He left, determined to fix this himself.

He found Emily in the library, studying. He grabbed her from the desk and hauled her to her feet.

"What did you do to me?"

"I don't know what you mean, Parker," she said quietly.

"You know exactly what I mean, this!" He lifted his shirt. "What the fuck is this!"

There were a few gasps from the other students, horrified by the sight of the holes that ran from the waistband of his jeans almost to his neck.

"Are you saying I did this to you? When we had sex?" she asked.

"No, you did something, some weird voodoo shit. I saw it on the video," he yelled, his face close to Emily's.

"What video?"

Parker opened his mouth, then stopped, realization dawning on his face. Emily let it sink in, then smiled.

"Did you make a video of us having sex without my permission, Parker? That's illegal."

He felt the burn of embarrassment and fear, and felt accusing eyes bore into him. Jail was a distant problem though. It was nothing compared to the horror he was suffering right now, and something his dad's lawyers would no doubt fix.

"Bitch, you are a witch or something. A bitch witch! You cursed me."

"A bitch witch, seriously?"

He let his shirt drop, aware of everyone staring, but Emily caught it and slid it back up.

"I think they're kind of sexy," she said, moving closer and running her fingers gently across his stomach and up to his chest. He felt a thrill at her touch, the holes pulsing, breathing their pleasure. He was horrified to feel himself harden.

"You're crazy! They're a nightmare, and you did it. You fix it, or I'll kill you, I swear." Parker took hold of Emily's throat. "If you kill someone who cursed you, the curse goes away."

"You learn that from watching Buffy or Charmed?" she laughed, sliding her fingers slowly into the holes in his chest. He gasped as her fingers touched his rapidly beating heart, pleasure and pain mixing, blending, churning, indistinguishable from one another.

"Please. I've tried everything," he gasped. "Doctor, specialist, everything! Please!"

"You haven't tried apologizing," she said, tightening her grip.

Paul Sheldon lives in Perth, Western Australia, with his wife, two children, and an aging dog. He works as an IT consultant, loves to read and write horror, plays guitar in a heavy metal band, and brews his own beer.

Chrysalis

CHRYSALIS

NICO BELL

7 A.M.

RENEE FELT the rush of blood between her legs.

Shit.

At fifty-two years old, Renee knew better than to leave the house without tampons, but her mind had been flustered lately as menopause toyed with her thoughts and emotions. Between hot flashes and eczema, she didn't know how any woman survived the transition. Renee wiped beads of sweat from her upper lip and checked her desk draws for an emergency supply.

Nothing.

She frowned. A knock on her classroom door caused her to quickly cross her legs and plaster on a practiced smile.

Milton, her boss and the high school's principal, strolled into her classroom, closing the door behind him. "We need to talk."

"Can it wait a few minutes, please?" She shifted in her seat.

"I'm afraid not." Milton frowned. "I'm concerned about you."

Cramps tightened Renee's uterus, and she could only imagine the sea of red she'd be forced to deal with when she managed to run to the bathroom. To make things worse, the eczema on her arm itched like crazy. Her nails dug into the toughened skin.

Milton cleared his throat. "I've noticed some changes with you. You're more distracted lately, and things have been slipping. For example, you missed last month's curriculum meeting."

"I had personal issues." She'd been an emotional wreck after sweating through her blouse and cardigan and trying to hide the pit stains from the glaring eyes of her snickering students. She'd decided to cut her losses, go home, and cry herself to sleep. It'd been decades since she'd felt so at odds with herself and the shift from her usual confidence caused a complete meltdown.

Milton continued. "There's more. Lately, you've looked more..."

She glared at him, silently daring him to use the words she called herself in the mirror.

Haggard.

Ancient.

Old.

"Tired." He met her stare. Milton stared at the spot on her arm she'd itched raw. "I'm talking as your friend, Renee. We've worked together almost fifteen years, and I've never seen you like this. It makes me wonder if maybe..." He took a steadying breath. "Are you on drugs?"

She barked out a laugh. "For goodness sakes, Milton. I'm going through menopause."

His face flashed beet red.

She huffed and looked down at the pile of skin flakes that had accumulated on her desk. With a heavy sigh, she met Milton's stare. "Sorry. That was too much information. Look, I know I've been a little off center lately, but it'll get better."

Milton nodded. "Of course. Well, if you need anything..."

He scampered out of the room leaving her alone to itch her dry skin. As she scratched, she noticed another dry patch on her wrist, and one near the crux of her elbow. Had they been there before?

One problem at a time. First, the bathroom. Then, the dermatologist.

4:30 P.M.

The dermatologist examined Renee. The dry patch on her elbow was now quarter sized, definitely larger than earlier that morning. Polk-a-dot rashes speckled her arms, angrily glaring up at her as they radiated a heat from deep within. Her pulse quickened and perspiration rolled down her lower back as the doctor finished the exam. With dwindling resolve, Renee forced herself to sit on her hands to keep her nails from digging into the hardened crusty flesh on her elbow.

"Eczema is normal during menopause." The doctor turned to the computer. "I'll put in a prescription for a cream."

"That's it?" Renee scoffed. "They're spreading. Don't you see?"

"That's because you keep scratching. Start the cream, stop scratching, and let me know how it goes."

Renee's shoulders slouched as she left the office and got into her car. She ran a hand through her hair. A clump fell out, and she sucked in a whimper as she stared at the mix of gray and brown. Her fingertips trembled as she traced the part down the middle of her scalp until they came to a clearing of soft flesh towards the back. Her throat tightened but she refused to come undone once again. It wasn't so bad. A low ponytail would be able to cover the bald spot. Still, she couldn't stop the tightness in her chest as she stared at the fallen strands of hair.

She decided to call the one person who always offered support.

"Mom?"

"Hello, darling."

"Something weird is happening to me. I'm not sure what, but…"

"It's okay, honey. Menopause can be overwhelming."

"I know, but…" The insatiable itch burned her skin. "This can't be normal."

"I know it's a little scary." Her mom's voice grew softer. "Go home. Lay down. Relax. I'll come over and keep you company, okay?"

Renee didn't think that was necessary. She was certainly old enough to take care of herself, despite the fact that her body seemed hell-bent on proving otherwise, but the idea of her mom there brought a familiar comfort. After all, if anyone could help calm her frayed nerves, it was her wise mother, who first introduced her teenage self to the wonderful world of panty liners and heating pads and stashes of emergency chocolate. The thought of having someone there who had been through it all before brought a smile to her lips. She let herself relax.

"Okay. See you soon."

11:50 P.M.

"I'm dying." Renee laid on her bed, naked, with the bedroom windows open. Perspiration soaked her body, and the blood flowed quickly and unrestricted from her womb onto the sheets. From the neck down, her skin was no longer soft. The dryness connected and wove a heavy armor over her entire body.

Her mom offered comfort. "It's almost over. You're doing great."

"I'm scared."

"I know, darling. I was too, but this must be done."

Renee tried to sit up, but the weight of the dry skin shell kept her on the bed.

"Tell me. What are you scared of the most?"

She sniffled back tears. "Getting old."

It wasn't just her body that marked the passing of time, but her life as a whole. She'd been telling herself she was middle-aged, but really, she'd be lucky if that were true. Life seemed to speed up ever since she crossed over into her fifties and with death suddenly a much more concrete realization, fear of the end had paralyzed her in a way she only just now allowed herself to admit.

But she wasn't dead yet. Her body may be growing into a new version of itself, but it still belonged to her. She could still claim joy and happiness and adventure. Those didn't fade away with the passing of time and she knew there was more to experience than wallowing in the darkness of fear and uncertainty.

The eczema hardened her eyelids, forcing her to close her eyes. She relaxed her muscles and allowed her body to sink into the mattress. Finally, Renee allowed herself to rest.

12:01 P.M.

Renee stood in front of her full-length mirror, peeled off the last of the skin patches, and flicked it away. The pile of discarded shingles sat to the side, a coat of armor now ripped to bits and waiting patiently to be tossed into the bin. Her wrinkles gently creased the skin around her eyes. Her hair, thinner but no less lovely, hung to her shoulders. When she raised her arms and gave them a little jiggle, the sagging skin flapped to the slow beat and warmth settled in Renee's core as she stared at her body.

Her mom sat on the bed, legs crossed, watching with a smile. "You okay?"

Renee let the palm of her hand slide down her aged breasts, along the soft folds of her stomach, and to the dimpled cellulite of her thighs. The reflection of her bright eyes in the mirror met her own and she took a moment to settle into herself. Air filled her lungs and she held it, closing her eyes to savor the sweet aroma of transformation, before releasing it.

"Yeah, Mom." She smiled. "I'm okay."

***

Nico Bell is the author of Beyond the Creek and Food Fright. She is the co-editor of Diet Riot: A Fatterpunk Anthology and Mine: An Anthology of Body Horror. Several of her short stories have been published in various outlets including Burial Day Press and Ghost Orchid Press. When she isn't writing or reading, she enjoys baking gluten-free cakes and playing with her dogs. Readers can find her at www.nicobellfiction.com and on Twitter, TikTok, and Instagram @nicobellfiction

ACKNOWLEDGMENTS

The first people I have to thank for this book are the writers who put themselves out there and submitted. It can be so difficult to risk rejection, and I want everyone to know that the quality of work I was privileged to read for this collection was top-notch. Thank you for sharing your stories with me.

There are so many people who have helped me make this book happen. First is my husband, who comes home from work so many days and starts dinner while I tap away on my computer, oblivious. He listens to me talk shop nonstop and never gets impatient or exhausted with me. He always has an opinion when I need one and is my first reader on so many projects. He's also my expert on all things horror, since I'm kind of a noob to the genre and sometimes have really dumb questions. Thanks, babe. You are amazing.

My daughter, Hazel, shaped so much of the art in this book. Her discerning eye and unvarnished feedback raised the quality of the covers by leaps and bounds. I ask her over and over for her help, and she's always willing to hop up and take a look. I'm a better artist because of her. She also helped me with the difficult final decisions of narrowing down the short short list to the final twenty-one stories. So if you just barely missed the cut, blame Hazel.

Jessie Grady is my person who will always talk through my problems with me, even if they wouldn't seem like problems to anyone else. Their advice is always sound, and anything I don't want to ask anyone else, I can ask them. They were one of the first people who believed in me, and taught me damn near everything I know about the trials and tribulations of self-publishing. I don't know what I would do without Jessie.

Tasha Reynolds is just an amazing person, and I'm privileged to call her a friend. She is wise and kind and helpful and everything you need out of a buddy when you are putting together something bigger than you are. Her proofreading, too, was so needed and so welcome. Thank you, Tasha, so much.

Cat Voleur is one of those people whose talent and joy in creating rubs off on you, and I know I'm a better artist, writer, editor, and just happier person for knowing her. Thanks for the late-night chats when I need them; you help me feel like I can accomplish anything.

Brandon Applegate has been a mentor and a help in damn near every venture I've made so far. His honesty, professionalism, and talent just ooze out. His willingness to format this book made me so comfortable that everything would be okay with that step; it's because of his help that this book has the polish that it does. Thanks for everything, Brandon.

Candace Nola didn't hesitate in her offer to promote and blurb and proofread and cheer for this book. A writer and editor of her caliber having faith in you is so valuable.

Judith Sonnet lent her name and credibility and AMAZING story to this volume. She didn't have to do that. Her dedication to bringing people joy with every project, her excitement about the craft, and her enthusiasm about lifting other artists up makes her an incredibly special person. Plus, of course, that crazy fucking talent.

Rowland Bercy Jr. is one of kindest and most humble people in the writing community. Working with him is a true joy. And his writing brought this book to a sick new level. I hope you had your barf-bucket ready when you read his story.

Truborn Designs' nw.reader has been an artistic mentor

to me when I know for sure she didn't really have the time. She so generously shares her amazing talent, and I would never have the confidence to be creating the covers I am if she hadn't nudged me to learn how to bring a vision to life. I have so much more to learn from her. Thank you, Kristina.

Oh my goodness, there are so many more people I have to thank. Everyone in this book, for your promptness, professionalism, and energy. Many of you put in way more than ten bucks' worth of effort, and I appreciate it. Everyone who helped promote on Facebook and Twitter. Everyone who pre-ordered, reviewed, and shared. And last, most simply, everyone who gave this book a shot. I hope you loved it.

ABOUT THE EDITOR

Ruth Anna Evans is a writer and editor of short horror fiction. She has published the collection *No One Can Help You: Tales of Lost Children and Other Nightmares*, several short stories, novelettes, and the novella *What Did Not Die*. *Ooze* is the first anthology she has produced. Ruth Anna can be found on Twitter @ruthannaevans, on Facebook as Ruth Anna Evans, and on her website at www.ruthannaevans.com.